Walking Where the Willows Whisper

The Sixth Little Wychwell Mystery

By

Stella Stafford

This novel follows the earlier Little Wychwell Mysteries

Did Anyone Die?

A Very Quiet Guest

All that Glisters is not Silver

Speak of the Wolf

and

Some People Go Both Ways

This is a work of fiction and entirely the invention of the author's imagination except that Oxford and most of the places described in it really do exist, apart from Kings and Coromandel Colleges. Little Wychwell and Upper Storkmorton do not exist in real life.

Any resemblance between the characters in the book and real people is entirely accidental. The author has no knowledge whatsoever about the work of secret agents, this is a work of fiction and entirely invented. But she got quite fond of Flipper in *All that Glisters is not Silver* so she had to let him back into another story.

A translation of the Latin and other non-English phrases used in this novel and the other five Little Wychwell novels is included as an Appendix to this novel. It is also available on the author's website at www.stellas-home.co.uk under the section for the Little Wychwell mysteries.

Chapter 1

Elodea had Theodora tucked, firmly if gently, under one arm and was using her other hand to hold the small hand of Amadeus and guide him out of the kitchen and into the front hall.

"*No*, Amadeus!" she was saying. "We can't play on your tricycle in the garden just now! We have to get our shoes on and get ready to go out, right now, because it's time for playgroup!"

Amadeus stood stock-still at this suggestion, opened his mouth, and produced a toddler wail of mammoth proportions.

"Don't be silly!" Elodea said to him. "You *enjoy* playgroup; it has all those cars you can ride in!"

She dropped his hand and, readjusting Theodora to a more conventional position, left him bawling in the kitchen and trotted out into the hall so that she could tuck the baby safely into her buggy.

"When I was their age, Amadeus," she said, with more than a touch of exasperation, "mummies and daddies looked after their *own* stroppy little toddlers. They didn't leave it all to their nonnas!"

She started to fasten Theodora securely into the buggy. The previously happy baby objected strongly to being put down from the warmth and security of Elodea's arms. She also opened her mouth and screamed but had no chance of being heard over the volume being produced by her brother.

Elodea fished a dummy filled with honey out of her pocket and jammed it into Theodora's mouth. Theodora stopped yelling and started sucking vigorously.

"I used to disapprove of dummies for my own children," said Elodea to herself, "but a time comes for all principles to be ignored!"

Amadeus was, by now, prone on his stomach across the threshold of the kitchen doorway, head and shoulders in the hall, legs and feet in the kitchen. He was drumming his feet up and down on the floor. His yells were getting louder by the second.

Pippy, puzzled and sad, sat beside him and patted him gently with her paw. But his flying limbs discouraged her and she dashed into the hall to find protection with Elodea. Elodea grabbed the little dog, fastened her lead on and hooked it over the buggy handles. Then Elodea turned back towards Amadeus.

"We can," said Elodea calmly but so quietly that one would have thought it absolutely impossible for Amadeus to hear her, "get some chocolate from the village shop on the way to playgroup."

The noise stopped abruptly. A red-faced, tear-stained, trembling wreck rose up from the floor. Amadeus smiled through a cloud of dribble and salty water.

"Chocky!" Amadeus said, and he got up and rushed towards the front door.

"Whoa! Shoes on *first*!" said Elodea.

His lower lip trembled. He opened his mouth. He drew in his breath.

"*Or no chocolate*!" continued Elodea.

The breath was expelled. The mouth closed.

"Put them on *myself*!" he said.

"If you want to!" said Elodea.

A few minutes later a ragged procession of Theodora enthroned in her buggy, Elodea, and Amadeus, who had his shoes on the wrong feet, headed towards the village shop en route to playgroup.

Meanwhile Angel, Elodea's daughter-in-law and the children's mother, was where she usually was at that time of morning: in the Maitre restaurant in Oxford. She looked neat and efficient. She was giving the day's orders to the next shift of lower staff at the Maitre, reproving, explaining, amplifying. She had now risen to the position of assistant restaurant manager and was in charge of an extensive food and beverage team.

Due to depression after his birth, Angel had always left most of the care of Amadeus to Elodea and Barnabus, and her postnatal depression following Theodora's birth had been even worse. It was better, as everyone agreed, for her to return to work. What a blessing, said everyone except Elodea, that Elodea, who loved looking after babies and small children and did not have a career, or paid employment of any sort, was available to step so ably into the breach.

Meanwhile Barnabus, Elodea's fourth child and the children's father, was at work in the offices of a bank. No one else in the family had ever been quite able to understand his explanation of what he did there but he seemed to be earning a reasonable amount of money now. Elodea often suspected that Barnabus did not really know what he did at work either.

Barnabus, Angel, Amadeus and Theodora had moved from their tiny rented cottage in the rather squalid Burrows in Little Wychwell, and now had a huge mortgage on a small terraced house in the Main Street. It was a charming stone property with tubs of geraniums in the tiny front garden and climbing roses and clematis trained around the tiny porch. It was also conveniently close to the Old Vicarage, so Barnabus could easily drop

Amadeus and Theodora off with Elodea every morning and pick them up every evening.

"Why don't you just tell them to look after their own children?" Agnes Grey had said to Elodea one day when Agnes had arrived in the Old Vicarage kitchen at a particularly sticky and exhausting toddler moment.

"They can't afford to pay the mortgage *and* get childcare, and Angel can't *manage*; you *know* she can't! Postnatal depression *and everything*!" said Elodea, wiping baby sick from her blouse and sitting Amadeus firmly back down on the 'naughty step'. "Anyway, I *love* to help out! I love babies! And toddlers!"

"Well, it be up to you!" said Agnes doubtfully, looking at the trail of destruction that a tantrumming Amadeus had just created in the kitchen.

"I'll clear it up in a trice! Everything is *fine*!" said Elodea, smiling with fortitude.

"I'll put the eggs right up *here*!" said Agnes, who kept hens and had called round to deliver a dozen eggs to her friend. "That way he won't be likely to reach them too *easy*!"

Elodea dropped Amadeus, face wonderfully adorned with melted chocolate, off at the Village Hall for his playgroup session. The helper took his little sticky paw firmly. Elodea dashed out through the door and slammed it behind her, just too late to avoid hearing his enraged roar as she deserted him. She did not feel at all guilty as she knew he would be perfectly happy by the time she returned.

Elodea relaxed. Although she would never admit this, not even to herself, two small children *were* a lot of bother, especially as Amadeus had a bad case of sibling rivalry and constantly competed for her attention with his little sister. Just having Theodora for the rest of the morning would be so much easier and more enjoyable.

Pippy was dawdling in a tired way so Elodea picked her up and tucked her in next to Theodora and then set off at a very brisk pace. Theodora, who had spent the whole time in the village shop exercising her lungs to their full capacity, was now tired. Her eyelids began to droop, close, then snap open every time that Elodea thought success was achieved. Finally, after five minutes they stayed shut. Her cherubic baby lips parted. Her body relaxed. She was fast asleep. Pippy curled up next to her and closed her own eyes.

But Elodea knew this peace would only continue while the buggy kept moving. She did hope she did not meet anyone with whom she had to hold an extended conversation as she knew that any stoppage would make Theodora jerk awake again, not just aroused from sleep but screaming in protest at the halt.

"I'll say that for you, you gorgeous little diddums," she whispered to the tiny, plump, reclining angel, "you really *are* a *Smith*! I know your brother has tantrums *now* but at your age he was much more placid. *He* must take after your *mummy*! I do hope he doesn't cry as often as she does when he is a *grown-up*! Maybe she does it to make up for not yelling enough at *your* age!"

Elodea thought what a lovely day it was today, and decided to take the long circuit. That would be two hours of walking, but Theodora would hopefully remain asleep, and then she could collect Amadeus on the way back. After lunch Amadeus could go for his nap upstairs and, if she went back to sleep again, Theodora and her buggy could perhaps be popped out in the garden in this lovely sunshine. Elodea and the buggy sped rapidly up the Main Street, heading out towards the fields and woods.

Chapter 2

Barnabus and Walls met outside Barnabus' office, secret conspirators.

"Does Yvette know you are here?" asked Barnabus.

"Entirely negative! Naturally not! She thinks I am having a working lunch!" replied Walls.

"What if she finds out?" asked Barnabus.

"Well, I shall be very contrite and explain that I completed the task ahead of schedule and chanced to bump into you!" replied Walls.

"Don't you *want* to have lunch with her?" asked Barnabus.

"Yes, yes! But not *every day*! Some days I need a timeout, have a 'guys only' lunch!" said Walls.

Barnabus giggled.

"What is so hilarious, Buffy?" asked Walls.

"Seeing you brought to heel, old man!" said Barnabus. "Never thought it would happen!"

"You thought I would *never* fall for anyone?" answered Walls, with a sigh. "Did you think I was *so* shallow? I adore Yvette! As you well know! But that doesn't mean I want to be with her twenty-four seven! Not always! I still need to be Peter Pan sometimes. Yvette is grown up *all* the time. She just doesn't understand that part of me is always a kid! I worship the ground she walks on! You *know* I do! But I require some *different* ground sometimes!"

"*Walls*!" said Barnabus, really shocked. "You aren't already looking at *different ground*? You've only been married for three months!"

"*Buffy*!" said Walls, reproachfully. "Not the ground someone *else* is walking on! I need to see ground that *no one* is walking on sometimes, that's all! No one except *me*, *just* me, oh, yeah, excepting *you*!"

"I can enjoy the occasional little escape from domesticity myself!" said Barnabus.

With slight variations the two of them had had the same conversation every Wednesday since Walls had returned from his honeymoon in the Caribbean. Every Wednesday lunchtime they then both purchased exactly the same baguettes from exactly the same sandwich bar and set off together to eat them while sitting on the same bench on the banks of the Cherwell. The only variation consisted in whether or not they put their umbrellas up while eating.

Rain was falling in a determined if steady way. It was out of term and, due to the teeming rain, the river was free from boats. The towpath was empty. The willows swayed in the breeze, whispering soothingly to the two escapees from domestic bliss.

They reached their bench, at a point beyond the distance that most wanderers from the city centre ever bothered to reach. This section of the river was always quiet but in today's weather it was entirely deserted save for Barnabus and Walls. The wooden bars of the seat were darkened with water, and damp to the touch. Barnabus took out two fresh cotton handkerchiefs, used one to dry his end of the seat fastidiously, then produced a couple of folded sheets of newspaper from his pocket and spread them on the bench, laid the second handkerchief flat on top of the newspaper and, finally, sat down. Walls giggled, as he always did when Barnabus made such a performance about the seat being wet.

"I've told you enough times, Walls," said Barnabus, "I have to go back into work this afternoon. I can't go back in with soaking wet trousers!"

Walls ignored him and perched on the seat back, resting his feet on the seat, as he always did, whether the weather was wet or dry.

"You'll have the whole thing over!" protested Barnabus, as he did every week.

"Hogswash, Buffy!" said Walls.

The formalities of acquiring lunch and sitting down were now completed satisfactorily. They both relaxed and began to eat in companionable silence.

After the first few bites Barnabus paused.

"Doesn't this scene just remind you of 'There Is a Tavern in the Town'?" he asked.

"No," said Walls, through a mouthful of partly chewed bread. "Which tavern in the town?"

"Not a *real* tavern; it's a *song*. And it's not the *tavern* it makes me think about, just the line from the song. 'I'll hang my harp on a weeping willow tree, and may the world go well with thee!'" carolled Barnabus.

"Well with thee!" sang Walls, after him, *basso profundo*.

They both guffawed.

"I don't know why willows are always associated with mourning and disaster," said Barnabus. "I suppose it comes of being called weeping willows. But they are such lovely trees. They make me think of all the good times we had rowing, and the summer sunshine! Look at them, all green and gold. Have you seen the new growth in spring? Finest, purest gold. And the long elegant leaves, the way they sway, always moving, always whispering together. What do you think they are talking about?"

"Nothing!" said Walls. "They are trees, Buffy, simply trees! Trees do not hold board meetings! Board meetings, get it? Boom boom!"

Barnabus was used to Walls quashing his flights of fancy so he took no notice. He took a huge bite from his baguette and chewed it with enthusiasm and enjoyment.

"While no other ears in the world can hear us, how did our Marius pull that one off?" asked Walls.

"What one off?" said Barnabus.

"Don't be airheaded with me!" Walls replied. "Come on! You know which one!"

"No," said Barnabus, aggravatingly, "I don't!"

"For ****s sake, Buffy!" expostulated Walls. "You must recollect that he just got probation for six months. As did Dave!"

"Seemed reasonable to me for the crimes committed," said Barnabus, "especially given that they were both drunk at the time they committed them."

"Drunkenness is no excuse in the eyes of the law," said Walls. "Come off it, Buffy! I seem to recall that Marius managed to convince both the police and the court that he and Daniel were strolling along through the woods, late at night, having imbibed overmuch liquor. They then stumbled across a body lying upon the local dolmen. Being so intoxicated with the demon liquor they both decided to bury it, it being dead. Daniel was, regrettably, so affected by this distressing event that he then stabbed himself with an ancient dagger that he happened to keep in his room at home. However, Marius had been so very intoxicated at the time that on the following morning and for many many days to come he had no recollection of what had happened on their little night stroll. Then in a sudden moment the events all recurred to him. Naturally his first action was to rush back to the woods to find out if the body was still buried where they had left it… naturally, for he needed to do this to discover if his regained flashback was just a false memory. By an extraordinary coincidence of fate he thereupon met you throwing up due to finding a severed hand; me feeling anxious about you; and, by a weird coincidence, Dave, who was on a very similar mission to Marius. However, Dave had come there to hunt for a body which he and his brother had accidentally deposited upon the said dolmen and which, as had suddenly occurred to Dave, might require further action as it is no longer normal in this epoch to deposit bodies upon, or even within, dolmens."

"Stilletto!" Barnabus corrected. "Not dagger. Daggers and stilettos are not the same. I don't see why you are having any trouble with that account. But you missed miles and miles of the story out. Marius and Daniel found the body and then decided to bury it, but Daniel got in a panic in case it was not actually dead. His state of drunkenness was sufficient to make him very pigheaded on this subject, so he got out an antique stiletto, which he had in his pocket as he had been showing it to Marius, who might have wanted to use it on a music cover, and stabbed the body through the heart. After that he was happy to bury it, although Daniel then became convinced that he had committed a murder. Marius thought he had convinced him otherwise, but clearly not. The thought returned later, which is why he committed suicide, one has to presume. Anyway, Marius and Daniel continued their moonlit stroll and found the scarecrow in the field. Daniel was quite convinced that the scarecrow was a beautiful girl, picked it up and started dancing round the field with it. At this point Marius wandered off home and never saw Daniel alive again. It's a fair enough story as far as I can see. Could have happened to anyone. Marius has my sympathies. If I drank alcohol it could have happened to me! There but for the grace of God go I! Or anybody! Made a change for someone else to find a body in Little Wychwell before I did. Although I went and found it later on anyway, as you know –"

"Buffy!" interrupted Walls, quite shocked. "You don't have to prevaricate to me! You know that's all fabricated! Have you lost your mind? *You know I know what really happened*!"

"I thought Marius' evidence was perfectly clear and lucid! And the sentence was quite in keeping with the fundamentally non-criminal nature of his crime," said Barnabus, apparently unmoved by Walls' suggestions. He pursed his lips firmly together and did not look at Walls.

"OK, OK, if you *want* to kid around, *do*!" Walls continued, after a few seconds of total silence. "Now let's examine the evidence according to Dave, Curtis and Sarah. According to his statement in court Dave had been called out to Oxford to assist his brother Curtis, whose girlfriend appeared to have most unfortunately accidentally poisoned her live-in lover. She had done this with toadstools which she had picked in the local Little Wychwell woods when on a romantic walk with Curtis, with whom she was two-timing Elton, both she and Curtis believing that the said toadstools were edible mushrooms. Sarah decided to make a tasty pot of them for Elton because she felt guilty about having been out on a surreptitious afternoon with Curtis. Elton was a violent man, who beat her and the children up frequently, which was why she had not left him – she was afraid of the consequences for herself and Curtis and the children. Right, so Elton attacked her after eating dinner and getting stomach pains, and she hid with the children in the bathroom in fear and trembling. When she came out of the bathroom Elton was well beyond the help of any medics. I will concede that my last two statements were entirely true. Guessing that the mushrooms were not what she had thought, Sarah then lost her mind with fear and distress, as anyone might. When she told Curtis what had happened they both failed to remember what one *should* do in the case of accidental death, due to shock, and Curtis offered to dispose of said accidentally poisoned body. Now not just Marius and Daniel but also Dave were several sheets to the wind with alcohol that evening. Clearly all the natives from your patch are prone to imbibe overmuch."

"Lots of English people drink too much. It's not at all unusual!" protested Barnabus, as Walls stopped to take breath.

"I will concede that point too," said Walls. "To continue. Dave, being asked to assist Sarah and Curtis, also lost his head entirely about what one should do with an accidentally dead person, and agreed to help dispose of said corpse. He and Curtis took it to the Little Wychwell woods, thinking to bury it somewhere it would never be discovered. However, due to alcohol intake prior to collecting the body – although apparently Dave was most definitely below the limit for drunken driving charges – followed by their further intake of alcohol to gain Dutch courage after arriving at the woods with a corpse, the burial never took place. Instead they absent-mindedly deposited Elton upon the dolmen in the very position where Marius and Daniel were later doomed to find him. They then drank some more to drown their sorrows, and due to the now massive intake of said intoxicating liquor the entire incident vanished from their memories. Sarah did not remind them of the incident but held her own tongue, for fear of the consequences if her manslaughter should be made public, and told Curtis and Dave that Elton had left her. Then she moved in with Curtis and all seemed happiness for a while. But, *soft*, as Shakespeare would say, *as matters chanced*, Dave happened to *also* suddenly recall all these events on the very dark and fateful evening that found you, me and Marius advancing upon the dolmen. Dave, being struck all of a heap by the unsuitability of the dolmen as a place to conceal a body, thereupon set off to find out what had happened to it subsequent to him abandoning it there. An interesting psychiatric phenomenon in which Marius and Dave both imbibed memory-wiping quantities of alcohol on the same night, and both regained their memories on the same night, don't you reckon?"

"Can't see anything wrong with that myself! It's the local village scrumpy, you know. Very strong! Goes straight to people's heads. It is only the fact that *I* don't drink alcoholic beverages that makes me immune to its effects! *Interesting though*, as you say! The memory recovery time being identical in two people! Perhaps Experimental Psychology would like to do some experiments and see if this result is repeatable?" said Barnabus.

"Buffy," exploded Walls, "they *didn't* both lose their memories and regain them on the same night! You know that as well as I do! *Or perhaps you don't*! For you seem to be experiencing a bad attack of amnesia yourself! Have you been sampling the local brew as well? Or could you also have had an intake of local fungi? The *dancers*! The *boggart dancers*! How the **** did their existence get kept out of court?"

"*What* dancers?" asked his friend, apparently guilelessly.

"*Buffy*," cried Walls, "this isn't funny! I want to talk about what actually happened! Stop goofing around like this!"

Then the truth occurred to Walls. He continued, "*So*! *That's* it! You've *joined* them, haven't you? You *are* one of the dancers! How could you? Flee this secret cult before it transforms your loyalties any further! How can you sit there telling me barefaced lies just to stay in with the in-crowd when the in-crowd is a crowd of loony village dancers? Don't tell me that the absence of mention of the dancers in court wasn't a funny handshake and apron job! I bet most of those oh-so-respectable dancers are in that *other* club as well!"

But Barnabus did not reply. He just sat there, blank-faced.

Walls glared at him. "Are you still my friend? Don't I count for diddly-squat these days? Surely being a dancer doesn't matter to you more than *our friendship*? Have they brainwashed you? OK, OK, at least admit *one* thing to me! *Admit you're one of them*! *Admit* you're a dancer!"

Barnabus giggled. "*Obviously not*. For there *are* no dancers. And you are entirely wrong about the apron and handshake, dear boy! Nothing to do with that." He continued, in a patronising way, "No, the reason that there are no dancers is that events are only constructed by words, and thus if there are no words about them, they do not exist. Ask Yvette! It was thus unnecessary to conceal the existence of something that is not there, and never has been there."

"I see!" said Walls, sarcastically. "I do not think, therefore I am not. *Non cogito non ergo sum*. The entire of Little Wychwell *non cogitos* and the dancers *non ergo sunt*."

Barnabus laughed out loud but it was a happy and friendly laugh. "Aunty Pris," he said, "would have an absolute fit if she had heard you say that! Talk about butchered Latin!"

"I don't see why," said Walls, entirely seriously. "I changed *sum* to *sunt*!"

"Languages never were your strong point," said Barnabus, with a sigh. "But to get back to the subject of the recent trial, I like your self-righteous attitude about any evidence presented being less than honest. You know perfectly well that *you're* the one who financed the best defence barristers in the country to get the entire set of defendants off the hook!"

"I need not ask how you knew that information," said Walls. "In Little Wychwell 'You never know who may be listening.'"

"That," replied Barnabus, "is obvious! In Little Wychwell not only do *you* have ears, Walls my friend, but so do doorknobs, stones, trees and the very air itself! And, most of all, Mrs Wigley has ears that are trained to hear a whisper anywhere in the entire parish. However, give me a little credit for my own intellect. It was perfectly obvious that they had not been able to afford them themselves, and the suggestion that such high-powered advocates were giving their time for love in the interests of justice for the oppressed was clearly nonsense. However, there are many many rumours about who funded the barristers, even though the rumour about you probably ranks top of the list. Alternative and much wilder rumours include the fact that while Marius and Daniel were burying Elton they found a hidden hoard of gold. Clearly this was used by Marius to pay for the legal team, but he remains as rich as Croesus and is just keeping quiet about it. There is a variant on this rumour, which says that after discovering the buried gold, by now referred to as the Boggart's Gold, there was then a dispute between Marius and Daniel as to how much each of them got, and Marius killed Daniel so he could keep it all for himself. This is a rumour that has more popularity in Upper Storkmorton than in Little Wychwell, I should add."

"Given your super intelligence it should be clear to you that not only did I supply the attorneys, but that it was necessary and essential for me to do so," said Walls, "for the sake of my rapidly expanding music shop empire. Marius is an *ace* store manager and sales guy. Or rather branch manager and sales guy *trainer* these days. I've opened *another* store! In Swindon this time! Oxford, Reading, Swindon! My pa is in raptures over my burgeoning entrepreneurial career! I haven't been this much in his good eye for yonks! He *really* thinks I am about to *abandon* academia and take a punt at trading next!"

"So, you need *Marius* more than *truth, virtue and honesty*! But *Dave*?" said Barnabus.

"Dave is one of *my* guys too, *as* you know!" said Walls. "Dave's doing great guns in the music store business! He's, er, he's got a very important post in the stock shifting area. Come on, Buffy; *both* of them deserved assistance! Where are your liberal views? They're good guys. *One* was saving his *best mate*, and *one* was rescuing his *brother*!"

"*And* Curtis and Sarah?" continued Barnabus.

"Dave *begged* me to get them some decent counsel as well," said Walls. "And Marius. And you *know* how persuasive Marius can be. I was unable to resist his entreaties."

"Precisely!" said Barnabus. "So you can get off your moral high horse and leave my quite legitimate and entirely legal leisure pursuits, *that I don't do*, alone! *You* should understand and respect the importance to ethnic minorities of traditional secret tribal rituals involving dancing and drumming that are part of their cultural heritage."

Walls gave him a mock punch.

"Don't be racist!" he teased. "But you were *broken* about not being asked to be in their frat before; *I* knew that. You were *sore* at being excluded, not being a Little Wychwell *Alpha Sig* or whatever! So I'm glad you got your desire. Should I really be saying, 'Be careful what you wish for'? You're confident this little dancing club is good for your brain cells? I am hoping that you are not partaking of the rave-fuelling fungi. Otherwise your grey matter will be in a state of rapid deterioration, for certain sure. Some mind-altering substances might be *legal* but none of them are *safe*. And while we are discussing that hick village which you insist on inhabiting, I need a translation of that word you used. What, Buffy, what is *scrumpy*? Sometimes I think I speak the entire vocabulary of UK English like a native born, and then another word springs up!"

"Cider," mumbled Barnabus, through a mouthful of sandwich. He was annoyed with Walls' persistence in discussing the trials of Marius and Dave and the issue of the boggart dancers. He didn't want to think about disturbing or awkward things. This was his lunch hour. Walls never understood about the importance of quiet lunch hours. Being an academic, his whole life was a lunch hour as far as Barnabus could see. Barnabus wanted to spend his break sitting peacefully and chewing his sandwich and talking about silly and unimportant things. Their current topic of conversation was bound to lead to indigestion for the entire afternoon.

"Ah!" said Walls. "You have an illicit still to produce this cider in the Little W? Like poteen?"

"Not a *still*, Walls, a *press*. A cider *press*! First you press the apples and then you ferment them. Mrs Longbottom started making it a few years ago as a sort of cottage industry, and it's been expanding ever since. And it's entirely legal. 'Little Wychwell Cider, a taste of the countryside!'"

"I wasn't aware that the countryside was so alcoholic!" said Walls.

"Only around Little Wychwell! Our bit tastes particularly intoxicating!" joked Barnabus, hoping that Walls was now back to only discussing trivial topics.

But Walls had not finished with the topic of the boggart dancers yet. He found the whole concept ludicrous and, although he had realised that Buffy felt insulted by the failure of the dancers to ask him to join them earlier, he could not, for the life of him, imagine why *any* sane person would *want* to be a boggart dancer.

"So," Walls persisted, returning to the subject with a giggle, "you've joined *them*? Ain't that cute! 'Somewhere deep in the Little Wychwell woods, a set of men and their scarecrow will always be playing!'"

"Didn't know you were an A. A. Milne fan," said Barnabus, irritably.

"Yvette discovered that I had *never* read *Winnie the Pooh* or *The House at Pooh Corner*. She has been reading them to me at bedtime. We are on to *Now We Are Six* now," said Walls, very seriously.

Barnabus, making a tremendous and heroic effort, managed to keep a straight face, despite the appalling vision this had conjured up. He also prevented himself from snapping that he would have thought Yvette would have classified these books as Ideologically Unsound Western White Male Dominated Discourses. Instead he made a non-committal sort of sound which was a cross between an 'um' and an 'ah', and awarded himself a virtual medal for exceptional gallantry in the face of overwhelming odds.

"*Hated* that ending though. Wish I hadn't reminded myself of it now. Had me in *absolute floods*!" said Walls.

"Does that to me these days too!" said Barnabus. "Didn't bother me at all when I was younger, but *now*! '*But wherever they go and whatever happens to them on the way, in that enchanted place on the top of the forest a little boy and his bear will always be playing.*'[1] It's just too sad. Too sad for words! Worse than *Toy Story 3*!"

They both sniffed. Then they blew their noses, loudly. This shared outpouring of public grief restored male bonding and harmony. Both of them relaxed, turned back to watch the river flowing endlessly past them, and lifted their baguettes companionably to their mouths again. Barnabus had his jaws stretched for a massive bite when he stopped, lowered the baguette, and leaned forward to stare at the water.

"See that log?" asked Barnabus.

"Which log?" asked Walls, chewing happily on his own huge mouthful and thinking of nothing in particular.

"*That* one! Do you know? I thought, just for a moment, that it looked more like a corpse than a log! Silly me!" said Barnabus, pointing.

"Buffy! Buffy! Such a wonderful imagination! But you have stumbled upon quite enough dead bodies for one

---

[1] A.A. Milne, *The House at Pooh Corner*

lifetime already! It's a *log*! Or rather a fallen-in-the-river-tree-branch!" said Walls, having glanced very quickly and casually at it.

The log was drifting towards the low earth bank of the river. It was clearly going to bang into it a few yards below the place where they were sitting. The log was so sodden by river water that the overcoat it was wearing looked darkest black.

"Walls!" exclaimed Banabus. "The log is wearing an overcoat!"

They both put the ends of their baguettes back into the bags, put the bags down neatly on the bench, and then sprang forwards towards the river.

"Is there a branch anywhere on the bank? Something we can use to haul it in? Then we could see exactly what it is." said Walls.

"I think it's going to arrive by itself!" said Barnabus.

They were both still clinging to the hope that the object was, somehow, a log that just chanced to be wearing an overcoat.

"Someone could have hung their coat over a tree, forgotten about it, left it there. Branch snaps off. Result: floating log with coat on?" suggested Walls.

"Or someone could have taken their coat off and fastened their coat right round the branch to keep it on there, and then forgotten about it. Maybe it was windy, so they didn't want it to blow away. That's why the buttons are done up! The rest – as you said," said Barnabus, bowing slightly towards Walls.

But the object rolled slightly in the water, revealing that it had a face. There was no longer any doubt.

Barnabus groaned. "Not *again*! Surely not *again*! I suppose we have to fish it out? I guess we can't just leave it here. But *no*! Not police interviews again! Work are *not* going to be amused at all when I don't reappear this afternoon! I'll have to phone them. I just hope they believe me!"

"The consequences will be much worse than that for me! Yvette will find out about my escape to have lunch with you!" said Walls. "Let's just go back to the bench and both shut our eyes for a few minutes and let the thing float off again."

"*No*! We can't do that. You know we can't! What does it matter if Yvette finds out you were playing truant? What does it matter if I get the sack, come to that! Someone is drowning or drowned or something, and we are just ignoring their plight! What if it's alive?" exclaimed Barnabus.

"You won't get fired! You can get the police to explain if work doesn't believe you. You have not deceived your employers about where you are. No reason for you not to eat lunch on the towpath. *Yvette* finding out is what is crucial! She is going to be beyond furious! You will be pulling *me* out of the river next as Yvette will have no scruples at all about pushing me into it! It's not alive. It's obviously not alive!" replied Walls.

"Just avoid going near the river with Yvette for the next few days then!" murmured Barnabus. He was not really listening to Walls but concentrating on the flow and ebb of the body. It was definitely coming closer. Just a bit closer and they would be able to get hold of it and pull it in.

"And what if the thing is *decomposing*?" asked Walls. "I don't want to go near it! It will *stink*! What if it bursts or something? *I* might *puke*!"

"Walls," said Barnabus, heartlessly, "pull yourself together! You've studied enough decaying-body photographs in your research on twentieth-century warfare. Now you can compare the photographic evidence with a *real* body! Get some practical experience of your specialist subject! Furthermore, this body might not be *dead*. This *body* might be *alive*! Think of that! We *have* to get it out! Kneel down here and we can grab it together!"

"I like that!" said Walls. "*You* were the one who puked up everywhere *last* time we found a body! And you had had plenty of experience of finding bodies *before* that, whereas I had none!"

"*You* didn't find the body last time! It wasn't '*we*'; it was *me*! You never even *saw* the body last time!" said Barnabus, indignantly and losing all control of his grammar. "And it wasn't the *body* that made me throw up! *It wasn't even a whole body*! It was a *severed hand*! Entirely different! And I haven't found *that* many bodies either! You make it sound like I find them *all* the time! I've *only found three*!"

By now, despite Walls's protests, they were both kneeling on the edge of the bank and reaching towards the ghastly thing.

"*Three* more corpses than *most* people *ever* find!" said Walls. "And," he added, as the object came within reach and he very gingerly seized the sodden fabric of the overcoat, "it's *four* now!"

"Well you've found *two* yourself if you count '*our*' last one, even if you didn't see it! Help me heave the thing in and shut your gob!" said Barnabus, gasping for breath as they both pulled the body towards them against the current.

"Shut it yourself!" said Walls. "You are *so* unfit these days! Don't you have *any* muscles any more? You should start rowing *regularly* again! Now! Lift! *Lift*!"

"I *am* lifting!" retorted Barnabus. "It's the weight of the water. This thing weighs a ton!"

The body bumped backwards and forwards against the bank as the water played with it. They both heaved but to no avail. It remained firmly in the water.

"You aren't putting *any* effort in at all! And you aren't lifting at the *same time* as *me*! I forgot! It all comes of being *Stroke* for years. You only got that position because you couldn't keep in time with everyone else!" expostulated Walls, sweat dropping from his brow.

"*Walls*," said Barnabus, deeply wounded by these cruel words, "you can do *all* the lifting entirely by yourself if *that's* what you think!"

They both let go of the soaked material, straightened up to full height and glared at each other. The sounds of lapping water and the gentle if ominous bump of the body against the muddy bank continued at their feet.

After a few moments of staring at each other nose to nose Walls backed down, graciously.

"OK, OK! You got to be Stroke because you were the *best*!" Walls said.

"You were *pretty* tiptop yourself!" said Barnabus, equally generously. "You still are! I wish I *could* row these days, but, you know, children, and all that! No time!"

They gave each other a bear hug.

"All the same, you *can't* keep in time with anyone else! You *never could*!" added Walls.

Barnabus, whose sunny temperament had revived, laughed. "But, you see, I didn't have to. I was *Stroke*!"

Walls glanced down at the water. "Freaking hell! The thing's gone off again! Quick! Get in front of it!"

They both rushed a few yards further downriver and caught their prey again on its next sortie towards the bank. They got a firm hold on the cloth and tensed their muscles once more.

"Just a minute!" said Walls. "I've just had a thought!"

"How often have I warned you about excessive use of the brain?" asked Barnabus. "OK. Easy all, way enough."

They relaxed slightly, only retaining enough grip to keep the body close to the bank.

"Before we continue with this venture," said Walls, "what am I going to tell Yvette? Because if you can't devise a good story then I am cutting and you can keep hold of this, this *thing* with one hand and ring the emergency services with the other!"

"Tell Yvette you had a headache, went out for some fresh air, just happened to bump into me on the towpath. Then we just happened to find a body. QED!" said Barnabus.

"Buffy! That will not take her in for one minute!" said Walls.

"Tell her the truth then!" said Barnabus, heartlessly. "She is only going to shout at you, at worst!"

"You always tell Angel the truth?" asked Walls.

"*Naturally*!" said Barnabus.

Walls glared at him.

"OK, OK, *usually* I do!" adjusted Barnabus. "You know how it is, Walls: you start off marriage thinking you will always share everything, and then you realise…"

"What do you realise?" asked Walls.

"That you need your own private life, a few little secrets, like you always had from your brothers and sisters, from your parents. It's how life is. Apart from which it's only like getting the children a new hamster instead of telling them the old one is dead. You *could* tell your partner the whole truth but a lot of it would only upset them and make them cry! And I don't know why you have to ask me, because *you taught me that*! *You*! The master of secrets, deception, double-dealing and multitasking your assorted girlfriends! *What's happened to you, Walls?*" yelled Barnabus, who was finding the strain of discussing morality while kneeling on a slippery riverbank and holding soggy material that was enshrouding a corpse becoming a little too much for him.

"I fell in love!" said Walls, very dolefully.

Poor Walls, Barnabus reflected: wings clipped, exciting bachelor days ended, brought firmly to heel. Then he pulled himself together.

"You should be glad there was any woman left in Oxford who loved you enough to *want* to marry you. If Yvette wants to kill you when she finds out about this she will only be in agreement with all the other women in Oxford that you abandoned! You should be used to being in that state. Now help me get this blessed thing out of the water!" said Barnabus.

"You are so right!" said Walls, brightening. "Even though Yvette is entirely opposed to marriage due to her feminist ideals, she *did* marry me! She adores me! I am a *happy man*! All right! I'll help you and then I'll think of something convincing to choke her off with."

Barnabus suspected that Yvette's feminist scruples about marriage had vanished together with her ideals that no one should inherit wealth when she had discovered exactly how much money Walls' family had. Barnabus had noticed that Yvette did not apply her principles to her own life with very much rigour. Angel and Barnabus had agreed that one could not choose other people's mates, but when they first heard that Walls and Yvette were engaged they were both anticipating an early end to the engagement. Yet the engagement had continued to marriage and, despite then changing their predictions to an early divorce, Angel and Barnabus had to admit that there was no question that Walls and Yvette were truly, deeply, madly in love – the strange attraction of opposites which could last just as well as the attraction of like-minded people.

"If we both get the timing perfect we *can* do this!" said Walls. "We *must* be able to do this! We *won't* be beaten! *Go, team*! I'll count us down. After three! One, two, three, *heave*!"

The burden seemed impossibly heavy. Their shirt buttons popped off as their chests expanded. Their faces were both set in grimaces. But finally there was a sudden squelchy gushing noise and the body rose from the water. They dragged it up the bank and laid it, face downwards, on the grass.

They stood there and looked at its back for a few moments while they recovered.

"A man!" said Barnabus.

"Unquestionably dead!" said Walls.

"Why?" said Barnabus.

"It just *is*!" said Walls. "Let's leave it there and ring for the emergency services!"

"We'd better make sure it's not alive. It might need the kiss of life!" said Barnabus.

"*I'm* not kissing it!" said Walls. "*You* can do that bit!"

"At least help me turn it over!" said Barnabus.

They turned the body over so that it was face upwards.

"*Quite* dead!" said Walls, his own face averted and his eyes closed so that he could not see the face of the corpse.

"If he *is* dead he hasn't been dead for *long*," said Barnabus.

"How would you know?" asked Walls.

"I watch crime dramas!" answered Barnabus. "I'll just make sure he really is dead. I'll see if I can detect any breathing or heartbeat or anything! And," he continued in a spirit of true heroism, "if it seems at all possible he's alive, well then, I'll have to try resuscitation."

Barnabus truly did not want to attempt such a task on this stranger any more than Walls did.

Before trying to detect any faint breath Barnabus gently brushed the hair back that was wetly plastered over the man's face. He felt a moment's pity for the poor lost soul. Then he gasped.

There was a neat bullet hole in the man's forehead.

"No need for resuscitation. There isn't any doubt that he is *definitely* dead!" said Barnabus.

"Praise be for that! I thought I might have to help you give another *man* the kiss of life! How ghoulish would that be?" said Walls, eyes squeezed tight shut and still facing in the other direction.

Barnabus looked at the face again. He gasped. Surely it *couldn't* be? He looked more closely.

"You don't even know the worst bit yet! We are in *big* trouble now! I am about to become Suspect Number One in the eyes of the police! Perhaps we *should* just leave the thing here and run!" gabbled Barnabus.

"I don't see any reason for you being a suspect!" said Walls, wondering if finding yet *another* body had tipped Barnabus over the edge of sanity.

"You don't know *who* it is, do you?" said Barnabus.

"No! *Do you*?" asked Walls, thinking he could hardly know who it was without looking at it, and that he had no intention of doing that!

"Unless he has an identical twin, there isn't a shadow of a doubt!" said Barnabus. "Of course I know him! That's why they'll think I killed him! *Because* I know him! They'll think that I killed him because I thought he was going to kill me!"

"Buffy! Buffy! You aren't making a word of sense! Who on earth would want to kill you?" asked Walls.

"A man who has already had to 'die' once because I found out what he was doing!" said Barnabus. "Can't you guess who it is *now*? It's *Ustin*!"

"I don't see how you can possibly tell who he is!" said Walls. "Drowning doesn't do anything for looks. I must take great care *never* to fall into a river. I *must* be a *beautiful* corpse!"

"What are you going on about?" asked Barnabus. "He looks perfectly fine, apart from being *wet* and *dead*! He can't have been in the river for more than an hour. In any case, he *didn't* drown! Have you *looked* at his face?"

"No, naturally not!" replied Walls. "You know anything to do with death freaks me out! I was merely considering the state of his *clothes*! Look at them yourself! What a *mess*! All dank and soggy!"

"Walls!" said Barnabus. "*Honestly*! He didn't drown, because he has a *bullet hole in his forehead*! Look!"

"I thank you, but I will decline that suggestion. I like to sleep at nights!" said Walls.

At that moment they were distracted by the sound of running shoes pounding along the towpath behind them. They turned.

A runner, who looked to be about thirty, was passing them, heading away from the centre of Oxford. He was travelling at a good speed but moving calmly and elegantly, breathing in a regular way. He was obviously a serious runner, not just a casual jogger. He had a Lycra running suit on and his wet hair was plastered down over his head. Presumably he had been running for a long distance through the rain. He was wearing headphones and Walls and Barnabus could hear the loud beat second-hand. He must be using the music to keep his rhythm. He glanced towards them but without any apparent interest. He lifted his wrist to study his running monitor and continued along the towpath without even breaking his pace. Clearly he felt that his training was more important than finding out what was happening on the riverbank.

Barnabus and Walls looked at each other. They both discovered the same thought in the other's eyes.

"You know," said Walls, "just for a moment *I thought that was Flipper*!"

There, it was out. He had said it. No possibility of retraction now.

"But, obviously, it *couldn't* be! That runner was too *old*. And Flip's dead! I *forgot*!" Walls amplified hastily.

"You forget how old *we* are! He *wasn't* too old to be Flip! But you went to Flip's funeral, Walls!" said Barnabus. "You know you did! How could you have forgotten that!"

An encouragingly odd reply, thought Walls. Not "Flipper is dead" but "You went to Flip's funeral". Walls decided to burn his boats.

"Buffy, old man, is it possible that there is something we *both* know about something to do with Flipper that *didn't* happen?" asked Walls.

"It is possible, but clearly untrue," replied Barnabus. "How could we possibly know anything that didn't happen? Naturally *neither* of us do."

They looked into each other's eyes.

"Praise the Lord!" said Walls. "You *do* know! I have been worried ever since the thing didn't happen that I would let something slip about it!"

"Equally!" said Barnabus.

They smiled at each other, a veil removed from between them.

Walls decided to continue and find out how many other things that had never happened were known about by Buffy.

"Audrey decided to go back to being a spoilt little rich girl. She stopped working and is affianced to a wealthy elderly senator," he said.

"*Audrey?*" asked Barnabus, completely confused at the conversational twist. "Who's *Audrey?*"

"You know, *Audrey*, your sister-in-law's sister!" said Walls, noting for future reference that he himself clearly still knew a lot more things that didn't happen than Buffy did. He added, to make Audrey's identity entirely clear, "Flic's sister!"

"The *plain* one? I remember her now!" said Barnabus. "But what the **** has that got to do with the current situation?"

"I thought you might be *interested*," said Walls. "It's the sort of thing Angel might like to know, hot off the press. I only found out about it yesterday myself from one of my back-home friends. He sent me a DM on Facebook."

"Is this really the time and place," asked Barnabus, sounding utterly exasperated, "to discuss *gossip*? Tell Angel yourself next time you see her! Right now we need to sort out this mess! Keep your mind on the job, Walls! We must call the emergency services! I'll do it. I've had enough practice. Not even any novelty in it any more. Like water off a duck's back these days!"

"I could call if you like," offered Walls. "They won't think I drowned him even if it is Us– whatever he is called. Come to that, *I* called them *last* time you found a body! So if I call now I'll be *equal* with you on phone calls about bodies. *Two all*!"

"*Ustin*!" said Barnabus. "And he hasn't drowned. I just *told* you: he has a bullet hole in his forehead! Just because we found him in the river doesn't mean he drowned! Could have died *any* sort of way and then been dropped in! No, *I'll* ring, and you can stand there and invent a plausible cover story for Yvette!"

"*Don't* remind me!" said Walls. "Good suggestion though. I will muse on the problem while you ring the City Kitties."

"For goodness sake, Walls! Don't call them that when they turn up!" begged Barnabus. "Or we will *both* be arrested!"

"Presumably I should also avoid fuzz, pigs and po-folk in front of them?" asked Walls, sarcastically. "*What do you think I am*? An idiot?"

"Usually!" said Buffy. "But I love you any way! Now do be quiet and let me get on with this call! I, er, I won't mention the bullet hole. I'll just say we've found a body in the river and pulled it out. What do you think?"

"I think that if *I* rang I *couldn't* mention the bullet hole because I haven't seen it. I really don't care what you say to them provided you get them to come and take it away so I can go and change my clothes, put these corpse-tainted ones in the trashcan, and go sit in a tub of disinfectant for a few hours!"

"Walls!" said Barnabus. "It's only a *body*! You row on the river all the time. I expect the water you get all over your Lycra is usually *full* of drowned-person particles! Let alone bits of dead rats and things like that."

"Oh shut it, Buffy!" said Walls. "I shall never row again if you say anything else of that sort! Get on with that phone call before we *do* get arrested for suspicious delay in reporting finding a body. I don't want to have to sit in a filthy cell waiting for my lawyer to get me out, and I definitely don't want to be forced to wear this ghastly gear for even *longer*!"

Barnabus gave Walls a friendly pat on the head, said "There, there!" sarcastically and then dialled 999.

Further along the towpath the runner seemed to be talking to himself. "That's *friends* for you, Sir," he was saying. "*Always* turning up just when you *don't* want them!"

Chapter 3

Elodea strode with the pushchair right up to the gate of the cow field. She stood there, looking at the peaceful cows lying in the grass on the other side and chewing the cud. Elodea liked cows. She loved their big eyes and their wonderful long lashes, their steamy breaths, their huge rough tongues. She thought they were very beautiful. She complimented the cattle on their looks while she rocked the pushchair backwards and forwards, backwards and forwards, to keep Theodora soothed and asleep. Pippy, who was now getting old and was curled up happily beside Theodora, was also fast asleep.

While absent-mindedly addressing remarks to the cows, who stared back at her and wondered what she was in a vague bovine way, Elodea was musing on something slightly strange that had happened yesterday. She had had a 'friend' request on Facebook from Fran. Most people would have ignored a request from someone who had tried to drown them in the Cherwell on the last occasion on which they had met. However, Elodea was not 'most people'. *Dear* Fran! she had thought, moved by the fact that Fran had made all the effort to search her out on Facebook and contact her. They must have sorted out her PTSD, and she is now *well* and *strong in mind* again! How *sweet* of her to look me up! So Elodea had friended Fran in return.

However, even Elodea had then thought it best not to mention this little matter to any of her family. She thought confidently that her children never looked at her list of friends on Facebook and thus would not notice. She had a most uneasy feeling that they were sure to disapprove of her friending Fran, and would tell her to unfriend her immediately. They would not understand that a long time had passed and that Elodea was sure that Fran was 'good' again now. There was no danger of John, Elodea's husband, noticing her new 'friend' as he never used Facebook.

But when she had checked her mailbox first thing this morning she had discovered that Fran had sent her a strange message. Fran had not put "Thank you for friending me!" or any other conventional reply used by social networkers, not even "Please like my page/buy my book/look at my video". No, Fran had sent a strange parody of Tennyson's Lady of Shalott to her instead:

She left the web, she left the mouse,

She took three paces 'cross the house,

She saw the water and that louse!

She saw his face, she saw his hair

She looked down to the towers there

Out flew the web and floated wide

The console cracked from side to side

"The curse is come upon me!" cried the Lady of North Oxford

LOL ☹ ☹ ☹

It did not make any sense at all to Elodea. But it did not seem very sane either. Elodea was wondering if the view she believed her children would take towards this new 'friendship' with Fran might not actually be the correct one. But Elodea did not give up on people easily. She remembered that Fran had always liked writing poetry. Possibly Fran thought that this variant on the original verse was *amusing* in some way that Elodea did not really understand. Perhaps Fran was using modern dialogue which Elodea was just not following.

Elodea had sent back a carefully considered reply:

Lovely to hear from you! I hope you are well. So nice to make contact with you again!

She felt this was suitable and sufficient.

Elodea's reverie was broken as she noticed that there was a woman on the opposite side of the field to Elodea's gate. She was climbing out of the wood over the stile. The woman sprang lightly from the top rung of the stile and dropped into the field. Then she set off at a very good pace towards Elodea along the footpath that crossed the field. A runner, presumably, training. She was wearing a red tracksuit that looked like expensive designer sportswear even to Elodea's untrained eye and... Now, that was odd: she was wearing red high-heeled shoes. Possibly a new exercise fashion? A form of extreme sport? Similar to people who trained by running in bare feet, only in the *opposite* direction of extreme? As the unknown woman approached closer Elodea realised that her long hair had begun the run by being piled on top of her head in a very elaborate style – the sort of style one might wear with the high-heeled shoes in an evening. Her hair was now rather dishevelled but beneath the wrecked style Elodea realised, as the woman came closer, that she was also wearing full make-up. Elodea looked more closely at the woman's face. Her children's assumed viewpoint on the Facebook friending of Fran was, suddenly and definitely, now looking entirely and horribly correct. For the running woman was unquestionably *Fran*. Had Fran only friended Elodea on Facebook to find out whether she was still living in Little Wychwell? The children were *always* telling her that she shouldn't put "living in Little Wychwell" as her job title on her personal information!

The question of whether the strange verse might have any meaning had also become horribly urgent! For Elodea had poor innocent little Theodora with her as well. What if Fran attacked *both* of them? *And* poor little Pippy! What if she drowned *all three* of them in the river?

Elodea calmed herself. She told herself she was being ridiculous. Even if Fran was coming here to see her – and there was no reason to suppose that she was, for Elodea had not expected to be at the stile herself till a short while ago, and even if Fran did write strange verses, there was no reason to suppose that she was anything other than a lovely person who was now quite normal mentally. In any case here they all were, in the open air. Anyone might pass by at any second. It wasn't the sort of place you could attack someone and think to get away with it. Elodea glanced, quickly and furtively, up and down the road hoping to see someone else, but there was no one there.

"Hello, Fran!" Elodea called to the approaching figure and was pleased to discover that her voice had succeeded in sounding pleased and friendly.

"Lode!" called Fran, slightly breathless. "Lode! You're *here*! How *wonderful*! This will save me popping along to the Old Vicarage!"

The Irish brogue had vanished and been replaced by an upper middle class North Oxford accent even though Fran still called her 'Lode'.

"Hello, Fran!" Elodea repeated. Fran was only feet away now. But the day had reverted to loveliness. There was *nothing* to worry about! Fran was *better*. She had clearly just been going to make a *friendly social call*! Maybe she wanted to say sorry for what happened before. Or maybe Fran had entirely forgotten about their last meeting. Poor Fran! She had had *such* problems with alcohol and drugs as well as the PTSD from serving in the army. Her long-term memory must be severely damaged.

Fran clung to the top rail of the gate while she recovered from her run.

"Slightly tired!" she said. "It's a long run from Oxford!"

"Fran, dear! You ran all *that* way! You must be *exhausted*! Especially wearing those shoes!" said Elodea. "Your feet must be soaking wet as well! Would you like to come home with me for coffee? I was just taking Theodora for a walk. You haven't met Theodora, have you? But I was about to turn round and go back now. I have some chocolate cake, or some coffee cake or scones if you would prefer! Then I can dry your shoes out while we have coffee. I could lend you some more waterproof shoes to wear going home. I expect we have something your size around somewhere!"

Elodea noticed that Fran had a skateboard strapped to her back. Perhaps she had not *actually run* all the way?

"No time!" said Fran firmly. "Just came to make *sure* you got the *warning*! Then I'm going on. Got to get back before *they* notice!"

Before *who* notices? thought Elodea, slightly nervous about that bit of the statement. Was Fran supposed to be in a secure mental health establishment right now? But Fran answered Elodea's question as she continued in her next speech.

"Confounded parents! They keep an eye on me *all* the time! Stuck in that room! I'd go entirely and completely mad without the Internet! They don't use it themselves. Frankly they have absolutely no idea what it does!" said Fran.

"Well, yes, I can see you need to get out by yourself occasionally!" said Elodea, wondering if she should volunteer to come round to Fran's house and take her out sometimes. It wouldn't really be any bother to do that. After all Fran's parents must be elderly, and she could see they would worry about her going out without them because of the risk of Fran feeling *suicidal* again. Poor people! She should have thought of that before. She should have contacted them and volunteered to help!

"I've just trotted over to make sure you read my message properly! I want to make sure that you *know*!" said Fran.

"Yes, yes. Thank you for the message!" said Elodea, hoping for further information.

"So you *know*! You're *sure* you *know*?" demanded Fran.

"Yes, yes!" said Elodea, in a soothing voice, as Fran seemed to be getting more agitated by the second.

"So tell me *what* you know! So I can make *sure* you know! Tell me *what* you know!" said Fran, with a cunning smile.

"I know about the Lady of Shalott and Lancelot!" said Elodea, reciting the original poem by Tennyson in her head, since she could not remember exactly what Fran's verse had said. "Tirra lira by the river!" she added, hoping this sounded very convincing.

"You know about *Lancelot*! You're *sure* you know!" persisted Fran.

"Yes, I know that Lancelot…" said Elodea, and she stopped, hoping that Fran would finish the sentence.

"*Jaisus*! You haven't got it at all, have you? He's alive; he's alive! I'm telling you!" yelled Fran at the top of her not inconsiderable voice and suddenly reverting to her old Irish accent.

Ah, thought Elodea. Clearly Fran was still very mentally unstable but she had developed religious mania as well. Elodea always felt that religious mania was a positive thing to have and must give disturbed minds much comfort and that "If they are not against us they are for us" was a very good principle to use. So now Elodea joined in with enthusiasm, giving the Easter Acclamation, but using slightly less volume than Fran.

"Yes, yes, I *do* know! He *lives*! He *lives*!" she cried.

"Good! Excellent! You have got it! That's it then!" said Fran, returning to North Oxford again. "Well, goodbye, Lode dear. I'm off!"

She turned abruptly and ran quickly back in the direction from whence she had come.

Elodea sighed. She did wish that Fran had agreed to come home to the Old Vicarage for a rest and some refreshments before she had left. It was miles and miles back to Oxford. She hoped she would be all right. Elodea thought about the brief conversation she had just had with her. It didn't make any sense, just like the Facebook poem. There was no denying that Fran was clearly still very disturbed in mind. But she had been very friendly.

Elodea wondered if she should run after Fran, stop her, insist that Fran came home with her, get her feet dry and afterwards give her a lift back to her parents' house in Oxford to make sure she was restored to them safely.

But Elodea couldn't leave Theodora here in the gateway in her buggy by herself, and she wouldn't be able to catch Fran up if she took Theodora out of the buggy and tried running while carrying the baby. Furthermore, Elodea was very sure that both Barnabus and Angel would be angry if they thought she had deliberately let Fran into the same house as Theodora. They would, with some justification, think that Fran was unsuitable company for their treasured daughter. Elodea hoped that no one else had seen her talking to Fran as someone was *bound* to report back to either Angel or Barnabus. That was the trouble with living in Little Wychwell: you never did anything without *somebody* noticing and reporting the event to *everybody*. Elodea looked around nervously but was pleased to discover that *still* there did not seem to be anyone anywhere near her.

Fran was clearly lonely, otherwise why seek Elodea out in such a strange way? If anyone told her she had done wrong they were entirely in error. One *should* befriend the friendless! Elodea resolved that when she was next on Facebook, she would send Fran a DM to ask if she would like to go out in the car with her some time. Or perhaps she could find Fran's mother on Facebook, if her mother used Facebook, that was. Fran seemed to have suggested that this was unlikely. Perhaps she could try and find Fran's mother in the phone directory and ring to ask her if she could take Fran out occasionally, as being stuck in a house all the time with her parents could not be good for any of them.

Full of these good intentions, Elodea did not turn round and go straight home but continued around the long walk that she had originally planned and arrived back, cheerful and well exercised, a couple of hours later. The radio was playing in the kitchen and she was just in time to catch the local news. Theodora would need changing and feeding as soon as she awoke but she was mercifully still slumbering. Elodea made coffee and sat down with her mug and a bumper slice of cake while still rocking the pushchair rhythmically backwards and forwards with one skilful foot, and half-listening to the news:

A woman has been reported missing from North Oxford. She is aged about 40 and wearing a red tracksuit and red high-heeled shoes.

There are still long delays on the northbound A34 following the police operation to remove a woman, who is believed to have been making a protest about the National Lottery. The protestor was travelling on a skateboard in the wrong direction up the outside lane of the carriageway. The protestor reportedly told passing drivers that she had to use the A34 to get to Camelot. A police spokesman said it was an extremely silly stunt and she was lucky to still be alive. Such action could easily have caused a major road incident.

Elodea felt terribly guilty about both these reports. Why hadn't she stopped Fran? She should have realised that Fran was in no fit state to get back to her home on her own! Thank God that Fran was safe in police custody now. Someone must make the connection between the missing woman and the woman on the carriageway very shortly. Then the police could take her home. Elodea wondered whether to ring the police herself and then thought there was no point as everything would sound ridiculous, especially if Elodea mentioned the plagiarised Tennyson poem. She might make things much worse for Fran. The police might think that Fran had been seeking out Elodea to try to attack her again when clearly Fran had had no such intentions. Talking to the police would also make it more likely that Barnabus, John and Angel would discover that Elodea had been talking to Fran and that she had friended her on Facebook.

Elodea concluded that she must ignore the whole thing. After all she might not have listened to the local news. At least she knew Fran was safe and that no harm had come to her on the return journey, other than being arrested.

Perhaps Fran had mistaken the dual carriageway for a single carriageway road and thought she was in the inside lane? Not that that would make Fran's behaviour much more rational. Had she been "floating down to Camelot" on her skateboard? The Lady of Shalott had died on the way, and Lancelot had finally seen her but not really cared much. Was Fran trying to die, *hoping* to get obliterated as she 'floated down'? But if that was her intention, then who was her Lancelot? With whom had

Fran fallen in love? Perhaps she had fallen in love with an ambulance driver?

Elodea crept upstairs, so as not to disturb Theodora, and looked at the message on her computer, trying to make sense of the poem. But the only sense she could make was that Fran was in love with 'Him'. That could be anyone for a mind as disordered as Fran's, even people she had never met. Lancelot could be a celebrity. But then why had Fran hunted out Elodea, just to make sure she had read the poem? It couldn't be entirely make-believe. So Fran must have seen someone from her window, someone on the towpath, someone she loved, someone connected with both Fran and Elodea.

She thought about what Fran had said this morning, trying to remember every word. Perhaps when Fran said "Jesus" she had not been calling on the Saviour, as Elodea had thought; that must have been a blasphemous interjection. Elodea repictured the scene in her mind. But in that case, who was it that Elodea must know was alive?

There was only one possible conclusion to this train of thought! Elodea heard herself scream "No!" out loud. This person *could not* be *Ustin*. Ustin was dead, long dead. Dead for years and years, deep under the ocean. "Of his bones are coral made," as Shakespeare put it. Unquestionably, he was gone for ever, as dead as Marley in Dickens' *A Christmas Carol*.

Perhaps Fran had hallucinations, imaginary friends! Fran must have imagined that she saw Ustin! Or perhaps she saw a real person who *resembled* Ustin and just thought that it was him.

The sun had slipped behind dark storm clouds outside, and the house felt instantly very cold. Theodora had awoken and begun yelling in the kitchen. Elodea knew that she must get up from her chair at once, move about, change Theodora and feed her, talk to her, sing silly songs to her, amuse the poor child. She must stop sitting in this chair having stupid and impossible thoughts.

Then Elodea saw the clock on the corner of the screen. She leapt up with a shriek as she realised that she not only had to change and feed Theodora but also collect Amadeus from playgroup. She had not got time to indulge in megrims and stupid thoughts! Elodea turned into a human whirlwind containing Theodora, changing mat, nappies, bottles, steriliser, baby milk and zinc and castor oil cream. Very soon afterwards she was zooming up the road towards the playgroup, with the buggy but without Pippy, to find Amadeus.

Chapter 4

"Mama!" said Barnabus, very severely, as he finally arrived to collect Theodora and Amadeus, who were grizzly and tired. He ignored both of them. Amadeus, surprised and upset by this rebuff, clutched his father's leg and started to howl.

"Yes?" said Elodea, feeling guilty and trying to look as innocent as she could even though she did not see how Barnabus could possibly know what had happened today. Perhaps he wasn't severe; perhaps he was just tired? But any hope of this faded with the next sentence he uttered.

"Why did you friend Fran on Facebook yesterday?" he demanded, detaching Amadeus from his leg and swinging him through the air to give him a big kiss to make things better. Then he planted his little son back on the floor and returned to concentrating on his mama.

"Well, obviously, because she sent me a friend request first! I, er, I thought I *should* be friendly back! *Christian*, you know! How did you know I had friended her anyway?" faltered Elodea.

"We will return to that issue later. For now, let me continue through your chronicle of weird behaviour.

Why did you *meet* Fran for a *secret conversation* this morning?" continued Barnabus.

"How do you *know* I met her?" asked Elodea, after a millisecond's consideration in which she decided that denying the encounter had ever taken place was unlikely to work.

"Why do you live in Little Wychwell if you don't want *everyone* to know *everything* you do!" retorted Barnabus.

"OK, *who* told you?" demanded Elodea. "I didn't see anyone about! And *why* were my friends spying on me and reporting the facts to *you* instead of asking *me* face to face?"

"Mama, they were *worried* about you! You are an idiot to think I wouldn't have noticed the friending on Facebook because you have clearly forgotten the little feature where FB suggests that you friend the friend of someone else! It just *happened* to wave Fran at me last time I looked at my page, and naturally it also told me that she was *already friends with you*! Believe me, that was enough to worry me even *without* being told she had been seen with you! She is *completely insane* and you never know what she might do next! Furthermore, while we are on this subject, *did you hear the news at lunchtime?* " asked Barnabus.

"I have been far too occupied *looking after your two children* to have leisure to listen to the news!" countered

Elodea, hoping she sounded entirely truthful, although she felt terribly guilty for telling such a shocking lie. All this panic, Elodea thought, just because Fran had been arrested on that skateboard. Surely none of these well-meaning village busybodies thought that she herself was likely to join Fran skateboarding in the reverse direction up the A34? What did they all think she was?

"Come on," she said, deciding that counter-interrogation was the best form of defence, "tell me which of my friends grassed me up! I want to know who told you about me meeting up with Fran, which happened, I might add, entirely by chance!"

"Really, Mama, where *do* you get such *awful* expressions from? *Grassed you up*? Anyone would think you were an old lag! I'm sure they won't mind *at all* if I tell you who my informants were! There wasn't one of them; there were *three* of them!" retorted Barnabus. "Mrs Wigley, Mr Shipman and then the Vicar *all* stopped my car just now to tell me the glad news. Mrs Wigley *also* mentioned the addition of Fran to your list of FB friends, because she had noticed it as well. I expect she monitors all her friends' pages every morning! You're *quite sure* you met Fran by *chance*?" he asked. "Are you quite sure you aren't gullible enough to arrange to meet her in the middle of nowhere *in case she needed help*? Honestly, Mama, I don't know how we are all supposed to keep you safe when you go round doing such *idiotic* things!"

Ah, thought Elodea. Naturally, he was worried about my safety. No wonder he seems so aggressive. He was afraid I might have got hurt! But she was still angry with him so she yelled back at the top of her voice, "I can look *after myself*! I don't *need* anyone else to keep me safe!"

"*And*," parried Barnabus, as a clinching remark, "you should *definitely* not have taken Theodora with you to meet Fran! I just hope *Angel* never finds out about *that* bit!"

He was worried about Theodora. That explains everything, thought Elodea. Fatherly anxiety, understandable. But then she felt even more wrathful with him because of the suggestion that she would deliberately take her grandchild into possible danger. If Angel was so bothered about her precious offspring she should stop going out to work at all hours and look after them *herself*, thought Elodea.

So Elodea raged back in one long unbroken breath, "I *didn't* arrange to meet her; I was taking Theodora for a lovely, long walk while Amadeus was at playgroup and I stopped to look at the cows and there Fran was, climbing the stile opposite and sprinting across the field. I didn't even *recognise* her till she got up really close! By then it was too late to move away. The thing that caught my eye in the first place was that whoever it was climbing the stile seemed to be wearing a bright red tracksuit and red high-heeled shoes. You would have waited to see who they were too if you had seen that! In any case, even if I *had* arranged to meet Fran, which I *didn't* and most *definitely* wouldn't have while I was looking after either or both of your children, or *any* children, come to that, because I know Fran isn't always clear in her mind, but even if I *had* arranged to meet her I would have *had* to take Theodora because I could hardly have left Theodora at home *by herself*, could I?"

Elodea's lungs were now empty and she was forced to stop to take a swift gulp of air.

"Point taken, Mama," said Barnabus, waving a metaphorical white flag, humbly and hastily, before she gained enough oxygen to continue. "I'm sorry. I've had a strange day myself. I *know* you look after the children *really well*, better than anyone else in the whole world could possibly manage. Better than me and Angel ourselves. I *kno*w you do!"

Elodea nodded her head in a *just* satisfied way.

Then Barnabus unfurled his own standard again, rehoisted it and returned to his trench to resume hostilities. "So what *was* Fran doing there? *In the field*?"

"Fran *was* on her *way* to look for me. She *was* going to *call here*, which would have been much worse, so it was as well I met her where I did. I admit, I possibly *shouldn't* have friended her back on Facebook, and I only did it because I thought it was so wrong to reject the lonely! It wouldn't have been at *all* Christian to refuse to friend her in return for her friend request! Not *at all*! But it turned out she had only friended me so she could find out if I was still living *here*. And once she had done that she came to find me. Just imagine. If I hadn't met her at the gate she would have come round to the house instead!" said Elodea.

"But *why* was Fran looking for you?" asked Barnabus. "Why? *After all this time*? Possibly you have, *very Christianly*, cast from your mind what happened during your *previous* encounter with *that woman*. Can I remind you that she *tried to murder you*?"

"Yes, yes, I know she did. But only because she was so desperately in love with Ustin. She's had treatment since. She's been released to live at home now. She must be fine otherwise they wouldn't have let her out, and I'm sure they monitor her state. I mean she couldn't have looked for me when she was still in a secure institute," Elodea rattled out without a pause, "and I *was* afraid when I realised who it was, not just for me but *especially* because I had Theodora with me, but I hadn't time to move away *after* I recognised her, and as things turned out I was being silly myself because there wasn't any danger. No danger at all. She stood on one side of the gate, we were both on the other, she was perfectly friendly, she had only come to tell me something, and then she just turned round and ran straight back the way she had come!"

"*But what on earth had she come to tell you?*" asked Barnabus, still feeling cross at the risk his mama had taken while at one and the same time feeling impressed at how many words Mama could achieve without apparently stopping for breath. She really was *amazing*. Perhaps she breathed in *while* talking, like a rap artist?

"Well, what Fran said didn't make *any* sense really; I must admit that. Although she is at home I don't think she *can* be quite well in her mind even now. She seems to be very, very confused. She came to ask me if I had read the verse she had sent me in a DM on Facebook," explained Elodea.

"And you had? What verse?" demanded Barnabus.

"Well, yes, I always read *all* my DMs. Not like you, *ignoring them all*! You always ignore the ones from *me* anyway. But the verse was just a garbled parody of part of 'The Lady of Shalott'. It didn't make *any* sense at all; there was *no* meaning in it!" said Elodea, with her fingers crossed behind her back to avert this lie. She was not going to mention her suspicions about Ustin to Barnabus. Ustin was dead and thus he could *not* have been on the towpath. It was quite ridiculous to suggest he could have been, but it might worry Barnabus.

Barnabus said nothing so Elodea continued, "I think she must be just a *little* bit disturbed again at present. Not dangerous but not quite firing on all cylinders, you know. I expect her memory is permanently damaged from before – all those illegal drugs and alcohol. It's surprising her brain still functions! Poor Fran! What a *terrible* life she has had! No one could really take *anything* she says *seriously* these days!"

"I think the police might take what she says very seriously these days!" replied Barnabus. "You realise she's been arrested?"

"Well, yes," said Elodea, reluctantly, "I *did* hear that. I did hear the lunchtime news. I wasn't telling you the truth about not hearing the news. I was being very deceptive. I admit, I told you a barefaced lie. I'm so sorry, Barnabus! What a bad example to set you! But, while it was dangerous to herself and the traffic, when it comes down to it she was only doing silly things with a skateboard on the A34. She wasn't intentionally hurting anyone else. I suppose the skateboarding proves it. Her brain is malfunctioning. She really has no idea what she is doing at the minute!"

"It won't *just* be the skateboard affair very shortly! I am quite confident that they will shortly be adding a few more charges, including *murder*! You are lucky that you haven't been arrested as her *co-conspirator* the way you have been behaving today!" said Barnabus, pleased with the sensation he was achieving with this speech.

"*Murder*?" gasped Elodea.

"Yes, she's a *perfectly harmless* psychopath," said Barnabus.

"*Murder*? Impossible! I *can't* believe it! She *wouldn't* have done such a thing. *Who* is she supposed to have murdered?" demanded Elodea.

"Who do you *think*?" responded Barnabus. "Didn't she *tell* you during your *chummy* conversation this morning?"

He was furious again. How could Mama, who had been so nearly killed by Fran herself, assert that Fran *wasn't likely to kill someone else*? Mama took Christianity too far. She was *too* good and *too* forgiving. She really wasn't safe to be let loose on her own!

"No, she didn't tell me *anything* about killing anyone and I can't *imagine* who it was! I have no idea!" yelled Elodea, equally angry.

Elodea reviewed her conversation with Fran and had a sudden terrible thought.

"Unless," she mused, more quietly and soberly, "it was one of her *parents*? She seemed to be a bit annoyed with them for looking after her and keeping her safe in the house. That would be so very, *very* tragic. No, even worse, I do hope she didn't do such a terrible thing just to get out and talk to *me*. That would be too *too* awful! I'm sure if she did she can't have meant to do anything so dreadful. She must have just got confused and…"

Elodea's voice trailed off in an image of Fran bashing one of her parents over the head with a blunt object and skipping away through an open front door.

Barnabus looked at her. "You really *don't* know, do you?" he said, gently.

"No," said Elodea. "I already *told* you that! I *don't* lie to you! Usually! You *know* that! Except for the bit about not hearing the news at lunchtime. And I've apologised for that already!"

"Thank goodness you aren't shielding the horrible woman!" said Barnabus, speaking at normal volume. "Oh, Mama, I'm so *tired*. I've had such an *awful* day!"

She looked at her youngest, her *own* baby son, and gave him a big hug.

During the big and silent hug they could hear the wails of Theodora and Amadeus, which suddenly seemed very loud and very insistent. Theodora was protesting because she had been left in the buggy by herself for far more than thirty seconds. Amadeus was sitting on the floor and crying in sympathy with Theodora and also sobbing because Elodea and Barnabus were arguing. His whole small world seemed to him to have fallen to pieces. Elodea fished Theodora hastily out of the buggy and started to soothe her, and Barnabus swooped down on Amadeus, picked him up and played 'windmills' with him till he laughed again.

"So," said Elodea, when peace and harmony were restored, "tell me what happened today. All the things I don't know about! Why are you so tired? Who is Fran supposed to have killed?"

"I *can't* tell you now. I'm too tired!" said Barnabus, sounding like a peevish toddler himself. "And I still have to get these children home *and* feed them *and* put them to bed! And *then* feed myself! And *then* get all the *washing* done! At least I don't have to cook for Angel as well tonight because she's on the *very* late shift!"

"Do you want to eat *here*?" asked Elodea. "I have plenty of casserole because Dad rang and said he is taking a visitor out for dinner this evening in Oxford."

"No," Amadeus suddenly shrieked. "*Not* here! Want to go *home*! Go home! Go *home*! *Go home*!"

"But Dada would *like* to have dinner *here*!" said his father and then sat down heavily on the nearest chair.

Amadeus opened his mouth and began a splendid tantrum, throwing himself onto the floor and kicking his feet while screaming like a jet taking off.

Elodea looked at Barnabus. He *did* look drawn and exhausted. What *had* he been doing all day? Knowing she had met Fran could hardly have *that* much effect on him!

"It's all right, Barnabus darling," she shouted, directly in his ear, above the noise of Amadeus. "I'll take the casserole out of the oven and put it in a box with newspaper round it and take it to your house and then put it back in your oven. It will stay hot in the box till your oven warms up. Then I can *help* you with the children and we can eat together in *your* house. After that you can tell me everything else that happened today that I seem to have missed."

"Mama, you are a *wonder*!" yelled Barnabus, brightening up and gathering up armfuls of kicking, yelling Amadeus as he spoke. He balanced Theodora on top of the writhing heap of misery that was his son. Elodea collected the casserole, wrapped two newspapers round it and put it carefully into a cardboard box to transport it.

While she was finishing the casserole packing, Barnabus had a thought. He shouted from behind Theodora, over the sounds of the still-screaming Amadeus, "Could you possibly grab a tin of cake as well? I feel that would go *very* well for dessert!"

"Yes! Cake as well!" bellowed Elodea, to compete with her grandson. "I trust *you* have *coffee*!"

"Indeed, *yes*," roared Barnabus. "Coffee *and* wine, but you might like to bring some milk and bread? Oh, yes, and *butter*! I met Walls at lunchtime instead of going shopping, and *that* was the cause of all the bother!"

"*What* bother? *What happened?*" shrieked Elodea.

"Too long to tell you now!" boomed Barnabus, over the noise of both children. For Theodora, annoyed at being crammed together with Amadeus, was now competing with him.

Barnabus achieved a spectacularly gymnastic sideways bend and folded the buggy up, with a hand he did not have, added the buggy handle to his armful of children, and squeezed the entire ensemble through the front door. "I'll tell you when we get to *our* house!" he said.

* * *

Barnabus was quite wrong. There was no announcement that Fran had been arrested for murder or for any serious matter. Instead she was released, with only minor 'obstruction of a highway' charges that evening, and restored to her parents.

A week later the local paper reported the finding of the body but said that the deceased was a well known local 'gentleman of the road' who must have slipped into the river while in an inebriated condition and then drowned. The police said there appeared to be no suspicious circumstances surrounding the man's death.

"See!" Angel said, when Barnabus told her all about the "stupid" report in the paper. "This just proves what *I've* said all along! How many times have I told you that you and Elodea are ridiculously obsessed with Ustin and the idea that he might reappear. *You* have a guilt complex because somehow you think you were responsible for his death when it was nothing to do with you. He was just an evil criminal who ran himself into a final corner and decided to end it all. Come on, Buffy, my own dearest. The man *died years ago. Accept it*! You just *thought* it was him because you were overstressed. You were feeling guilty about sneaking off at lunchtime like that with Walls because he was deceiving Yvette. Not being totally truthful and honest *always* upsets your whole system. Then, on top of that, you had the shock of finding a body! So you just *mistook* the corpse for Ustin!"

"I suppose you are right," sighed Barnabus, *apparently* humbly. But he did not believe that he was wrong for one second. He had only agreed with Angel to keep the peace and avoid conflict. For he was entirely sure that there was more than the identity of the body that was wrong with the newspaper report. Even if the man had *not* been Ustin but just someone who *looked* exactly like Ustin, the body still had *a bullet hole* through its *forehead*. Barnabus was absolutely certain about that point. Yet the *report* said "drowned" not "shot and dumped in the river". "No suspicious circumstances"?

Humph! No pathologist could have failed to see the bullet hole and then, presumably, find the bullet and discover that the man had been shot *before* being drowned. There was also the matter of the jogger who looked like Flipper. That could just have been someone who *looked* a bit like Flipper too. But given all the other circumstances he thought that it most likely *was* Flipper. Barnabus was quite sure he could not have imagined *everything* about the entire event. So, something *odd* was going on – that was clear – but what could it be?

He decided to ring Walls and discuss it with him.

But, to Barnabus' surprise and horror, Walls said much the same as Angel!

"You have too much imagination, Buffy. This is the result of having an excess of it!" soothed his friend. "You see, your imagination has always caused you problems. That's why you were never an expert player like me; it's because you imagined all sorts of terrible consequences that would never have happened. I expect he had some waterweed or part of a *fish* or *something* stuck on his forehead. Just *looked* like some kind of bullet hole. Easy to mistake. Shock of seeing a body; could imagine *anything* with your sort of mind. This is why I had the sense to *not look at it*. Save me getting the horrors and joining you in wild flights of fancy! So the poor dead guy was a *drowned hobo*? Very sad. Or perhaps *not* sad. Being a hobo must be *perfectly* awful. Death could hardly be *worse*. The *clothes* they wear, Buffy. The *dirt*! I would chuck myself *straight* into the nearest river if that was my only career option! The guy had a designer suit on. It must have been *gifted* to the Simon House or whatever… *Pre-worn*! *Pre-worn clothes*! Couldn't take that! Absolutely *not*!"

"*Walls*!" Barnabus protested. "I *didn't* imagine it! I told you to look at the man's face yourself! You couldn't have missed seeing the hole in his forehead if you had. It was a bullet hole; nothing else looks like that! If you had just had the *stomach* to look at him you would believe me now!"

But even this insult was in vain.

"Buffy! You couldn't *seriously* have expected me to look at a *drowned man's face*! I would have had *permanent* nightmares! And, Buffy, you *know* you were under stress! I should not have expected you to join me in deceiving my wife. All those lunches. You simply can't cut being deceitful; it upsets your whole frame. And then finding *anoth*er body! How many is that now? Ten, *eleven*? I've lost count! *Naturally* you were not yourself. Maybe he had crashed into a tree branch in the water. That would be why he had that mark on his forehead. Enough pieces of tree floating around in the river! You just *saw* it as a bullet hole because you were *distressed*. Yvette says you *constructed* his appearance from your *own discourse*! Really interesting: discourse theory. You should take time to study it. She gives me the most amazing papers to read. Did you know that the patriarchal social order is entirely a construct of discourse? And that it can be only broken by applying better feminist discourse to constructs? Does Angel teach you about engineering? She really should. Anyway, must break off. Yvette's here!"

And Walls ended the call abruptly, before Barnabus could point out that he had *not* found ten or eleven bodies; he had *only* found four, as Walls knew perfectly well. Or that not only was discourse theory twaddle, in Barnabus' own opinion, but, as Walls very well knew, Barnabus had made a study of discourse theory as part of his own D.Phil. studies and knew a lot more about it than Walls did.

Barnabus was now thoroughly rattled and annoyed. Having his wife disbelieve him was one thing; having his best friend disbelieve him was quite another.

In the morning, when he trotted round to see *his own mama* to hand his children over, especially early so he could discuss the matter with someone who would believe and understand, he felt confident of sympathy and accord.

He deposited Theodora safely on the floor in her car seat and took the lid off Amadeus' bucket of plastic bricks for him. Then he turned to Mama, producing an *Oxford Times* from his pocket and waving it at her.

"Have you seen this article?" he demanded.

"I'm not sure, Barnabus darling. Which article?" she asked, slightly absent-mindedly as she was now sitting on the floor at the order of Amadeus to "build tower".

"Look!" he said. "The *Oxford Times*! This page!"

"Yes, I've got one somewhere, an *Oxford Times*. We always get one. You know that," she said, vaguely, adding another two bricks to the top of her tower.

"But have you read it?" Barnabus asked.

"I'm not sure whether I read it this week or not. If you want to borrow it you'll find it over there!" she said, waving a hand vaguely at the top of the kitchen table.

Barnabus glanced cursorily at the pile of newspapers on the corner of the table. That *could* be the *Oxford Times*, about halfway down the heap.

"I don't want to borrow it. I've brought my own with me. I want you to read this article," Barnabus persisted. Then he looked again at the top newspapers on the pile and his eyebrows rose.

"Are you doing some research, or is one of the great aunts or great uncles staying?" he asked.

"Washing machine keeps overflowing," said Elodea, casually, as she concentrated on keeping her now unstable and swaying tower under control.

"Go bang! Go *bang*!" crowed Amadeus, hopefully.

"No, no it won't. It's *not* going to go bang. Bother!" said Elodea as the tower fell.

"Build again! Build again!" commanded her little tyrant.

"What has the washing machine got to do with it? You are not making any sense!" said Barnabus.

"More absorbent! Quality newspapers are useless on the floor!" replied his mama.

"You shouldn't give people who write that sort of junk your money!" protested her son.

"Well, what else can I use on the floor then?" demanded his mother.

"Whatever! I don't know. Fix the washing machine! I have to go in a minute. I want you to read this!" Barnabus replied.

"An' I want you to build tower!" Amadeus said, in a competitive tone.

But Elodea scrambled upright, saying "When Dada has gone to work, Angel" to Amadeus, to view the page that Barnabus was saving at her.

"Yes!" she said, looking at the article titled 'Pig Poo Power'. "I remember now! I did read the paper because I saw that article. Isn't it amazing? Cyril is going to power the whole Manor House and farm from processing pig manure. It's a lovely photo of Cyril too! I thought at the time that you would find it interesting!"

"*No*," said Barnabus, "not *that* article! The report on the 'drowning' of a 'homeless man' next door to it! It's the man that Walls and I found. It says he drowned, not 'was shot in the head', and that he was a tramp and not Ustin, when we know very well he wasn't."

Theodora had now woken from her post-breakfast nap, which she always took in order to recover from being awake for most of the night, and was making stentorian vocal protests about being left in her car chair for so long.

"I'll be with you in a ickle tiddly minute, Angeldums!" cooed Elodea. Theodora ignored her and continued to yell.

Elodea scanned the article hastily. Then she realised that Theodora was now suspiciously silent. She whisked round to discover that Amadeus was trying to feed Theodora some of Pippy's dog food.

"Tio hungry!" he said, defensively, at the sight of his nonna's and dada's faces.

Barnabus removed the bowl of dog food and put it on a high shelf while Elodea held Theodora face downwards and emptied her mouth.

"No!" said Barnabus to his son. "Not for Theo! For Pippy! Not good for Theo!"

"Teo stop cry!" wailed Amadeus, at this mild rebuke. "Teo stop cry! Teo hungry! I look after Teo! You not care!"

He burst into a stormy tantrum.

By the time this little crisis had been resolved Barnabus was no longer early but late.

"So," Barnabus said, as he paused on the doorstep, to Elodea, who was now holding Theodora upright in her arms, the tiny head resting over her shoulder, patting the baby's back rhythmically and gently to soothe her, "what about that article? How could they possibly have written *that*? Did the reporter get it wrong? Surely the pathologist couldn't miss seeing a bullet hole? Ustin wasn't a *tramp*! You should have seen the clothes he had on! Designer everything!"

But to his staggered amazement Elodea said much the same as Angel and Walls.

"It must have been the shock, baby of mine!" she said. "You know, finding *another* body! Maybe the dead man had the same ethnic origin as Ustin so he looked sort of similar, don't you think?"

"Mama! Do you know how *racist* that last comment was?" Barnabus exploded.

"You know what I meant!" she replied. "I didn't mean that everyone from wherever Ustin actually came from looked the same, but there's bound to be some national resemblance, and drowning distorts faces, doesn't it? So you just *thought* it was Ustin, Darling, because he is connected in your brain with death and shotguns and things!"

"*I wasn't* mistaken, and he *hadn't* drowned. He'd been *shot*! And he'd only been in the water for a short time. It hadn't disfigured him at all!" retorted Barnabus.

"I expect the mark on his forehead was because he'd hit something in the water – a branch or a twig or something – or maybe hit his head on a bridge or the towpath edge when he fell in. The police pathologist wouldn't get the cause of death *so* far wrong! It must have just *looked* like a bullet wound, and, you know, the *shock*…" Elodea trailed off at the sight of Barnabus' expression.

"I thought *you* at least would believe me. *Et tu, Mama!*" he said, really hurt now.

"*Barnabus*," said his mama, "you saw what the report said. I don't see any reason to think that the police pathologist would make such a terrible mistake! A poor homeless man fell in the river and died. Those are the facts. It reminded me of poor, poor Jason. So young! Such a hazardous lifestyle! I do hope this man wasn't quite so young and didn't lead such a sad life before he died! We must pray for the poor man's soul and then try to put it behind us!"

"So what about the fact *Fran* saw *Ustin* on the towpath? That *poem* she put on Facebook! The one she sent to *you*!" he exclaimed.

"You can't take *anything* Fran does or says or writes *seriously*. The poem didn't even *mention* Ustin specifically. It was the two of us who decided the poem was about him. It probably wasn't about him. Her brain is so disordered there is no reason to suppose that what she had written meant *anything* at all. Darling, she was skateboarding the wrong way up the Oxford Ring Road! That must tell you what her mental state is like!" soothed his mama.

"Well then! *Why* did she come and see you? Why did she come and *warn* you?" demanded Barnabus.

"I think," replied Elodea, "that if you think about it more carefully you will see that the case is closed and all that is necessary for us to do now is to pray for that poor man and for all people who are homeless in the world tonight."

At this point Amadeus, who was 'being an aeroplane' round and round the kitchen table, managed to run his forehead into the corner of the table. Elodea turned hastily towards her grandson.

"I suppose you think I should stop thinking about it in case I get any more stressed and then see *more* dead Ustins! Goodbye. See you all tonight!" Barnabus shouted at her back view, and stormed off to work.

Elodea sighed sadly. Sometimes her youngest son seemed to be the same age emotionally as his own son. She kissed Amadeus better and sat on the floor with him to resume brick building while balancing Theodora on her other arm. She glanced quickly at the clock: not *too* long before she could start getting him ready and out for playschool.

Barnabus leapt into his car in a big huff. Then he smoothed down his own ruffled feathers and realised that there *was* one person who he was absolutely sure *would* believe him, *one* person who would find the whole tale as gripping and exciting and as *unquestionably true* as he did. But he had not even told her about the discovery of the body yet, not spoken to her since then, or for quite a few weeks before that either if he was honest. Not that this neglect would matter. She wouldn't mind, he assured himself. But how could he have forgotten to tell Aunty Pris about this latest corpse? It was sad, he thought, that having children and a job and a wife and being so busy meant that sometimes you just lost touch with people even though you didn't *mean* to do so. He thought of several other friends whom he had not contacted since last Christmas, and thought that he must make time to look them up, or at least send them a quick text message.

Circumstances for renewing old acquaintance with Aunty Pris were all in his favour. Angel had a week's leave from work between shift changes and had decided to take the children up to Newcastle on the shuttle flight the following day so that they could all go and stay with her parents. Barnabus waved them off early next morning, feeling remarkably cheerful about being left at home alone, even though he would miss them all very much. For this, he mused to himself, was now an ideal, child-free, opportunity to do a little poking around on the matter of 'drowned tramps' with someone who he knew would relish the opportunity as much as he would himself.

As soon as it was time for lunch Barnabus hastened out of the office, trotted swiftly round to Jericho and stood expectantly outside Priscilla's door, ringing her doorbell at length and repeatedly.

Upstairs, working peacefully on her latest research paper, bathed in sunshine from the window, Priscilla jumped slightly at the first ring and then, as the rings continued and she realised who it must be, she sighed. She had been enjoying the morning so far. But the doorbell ringing like that undoubtedly presaged an invasion by Smiths – nobody else ever punished her bell push in such a way. It was no good trying to ignore them either. She feared vulcanisation yet again but whichever of them it was outside would never go away till she got up and answered the door. "*Periculum in mora,*" she said, aloud. "*Si vis pacem para bellum.*"

Smiths! They were always so convinced that she was just sitting there, lonely, with no possible amusement, waiting for one of them to turn up and 'rescue' her from her solitary boredom. *Numquam minus solus quam cum solus*, she sighed to herself. She had not been 'vulcanised' by a Smith for so long that she had begun to think she was finally safe from their predations on her safety, time, energy and even, in the case of Barnabus, her possessions. She always seemed to finish up having to fund Barnabus' sustenance or house his fiancée or one of his friends, or fund an item that he felt would be a positive pleasure for her to underwrite since he was temporarily unable to afford it himself.

But, despite these apparently gloomy thoughts, she had a huge smile on her face as she pressed 'save' and 'close' and headed for the stairs.

Soon she and Barnabus were ensconced in the lounge with a plate of biscuits and a large jug of coffee on the coffee table.

"Has Mama really not *told* you about her meeting with Fran?" Barnabus was asking.

"No. You see, I haven't *seen* her for ages!" said Priscilla. "She's *terribly tied up* these days looking after all her *grandchildren*, you know! *Familia supra omnia.*"

Barnabus entirely missed the fact that Priscilla was hinting that Barnabus and Angel were making unreasonable demands on Elodea's time by continually expecting her to look after their children free of charge.

"Well, her time's not *that* occupied now *grandchild*-wise," he replied. "She only really has to look after *our two* these days because Elizabeth's are both at school and she doesn't finish up having Elodeus and Jasmine to stay *nearly* so often! And she never *did* have Sophie to look after because of her having nannies, you know!"

He took a sip of coffee thoughtfully and then added, "Of course it was quite a cheek of Elizabeth to *keep* sending Elodeus and Jasmine down to stay for weeks at a time until they got old enough for school. And she *still* sends them down for most of the school holidays!"

"*Quite!*" said Priscilla, *very* stiffly, but Barnabus again entirely missed the point. "Of course," Priscilla continued, "I have spoken to your mama on the telephone, quite often, but only in brief snatches before she had to end the call to deal with *little crises. Pueri pueri, pueri puerilia tractant.*"

"Perhaps she *has* told you about it on the phone and you just weren't paying attention?" suggested Barnabus, still oblivious of her crusade to get him to understand the burden he and Angel were imposing on Elodea's time and life. Priscilla decided to abandon the attempt. "*Barba crescit caput nescit*," she said to herself. "In any case, Elodea is so strange about small children. Possibly she *does* enjoy being enslaved by them!"

So Priscilla merely said, "I agree that that is e*ntirely* possible!" perfectly sanguine about this suggestion. "Elodea, as you know, does sometimes tend to rather *run on and on*, and just *occasionally* I do rather lose track of what she is saying, especially as I have so many *important* and *weighty* matters on my mind…"

"Quite *so*!" agreed Barnabus, tactfully, secretly thinking that nothing about Priscilla's work or career was really of any importance whatsoever. He *had* thought it was, once, but now that he had left academia for ever and was out in the 'real' world, his viewpoint had changed. "I'll assume you don't know about *any* of it, and tell it all to you again."

Barnabus began his account by describing his mama's recent encounters with Fran. Priscilla *appeared* attentive and even deeply impressed, but in fact she was only half-listening, if that. She managed to grasp that Fran had somehow appeared in Little Wychwell to visit Elodea but the rest of the story floated past her brain, which had already returned to her research.

Priscilla had, however, been working on her 'attentive look' for Senior Common Room meetings recently. Coromandel College had a new and relatively youthful principal, or rather, to give him his correctly venerable and ancient title, a new and relatively youthful prevaricator. This new Prevaricator of Coromandel had issued a memo reminding the Coromandel dons that attendance and participation at Senior Common Room meetings was vital for preserving the future of the college. In fact, such attendance was now compulsory unless you could produce a cast-iron excuse or a sick note. The memo had then added that in these difficult financial times it might one day become necessary to *reduce the subjects of study* available in Coromandel to only those which could demonstrate their *immediate and provable* financial worth to the industrial and economical forces of Britain. Priscilla, being a Classics don, had been enraged and insulted by this memo but, having spent years coping with the little ego trips of previous prevaricators and not at all wishing to become unemployed, she had resolved to work on *appearing* to be fascinated, enthusiastic and enraptured by the pursuit of the Senior Common Room meeting agenda. She did not want to risk her post being not retained lest the further loss of any Coromandel millions in Eurozone investments should perchance lead to cuts in staffing levels. She had spent a morning practising suitable facial expressions in front of her own mirror, then practising retaining them while thinking of other things, and this had clearly paid dividends even if it did give her the effect of having used botox. She was pleased to discover that the effect was definitely working on Barnabus who, having known her for years, was much more likely to notice that she was not paying any attention to what he was saying than was the Prevaricator of Coromandel.

But there was a fault in her plan. Unlike a college meeting, in which someone else might respond to the speaker, she was supposedly in a one-to-one conversation with Barnabus. She suddenly realised that there was silence in the room. Barnabus' account had, clearly, come to a halt and someone else must reply. Furthermore, there was only her available to do so. Priscilla leapt boldly into the breach with what she trusted was a suitable statement, in fact *more* than suitable. She felt enchanted with her own prowess in rapid and brilliant invention, as demonstrated by her reply.

"So," Priscilla said, "I see. How *very* interesting. So, to *summarise*, Fran is *back in custody* now, I *presume*? *Qui totum vult totum perdit!*"

"No, no!" said Barnabus. "Of course not! She wasn't doing anything *very* illegal; I just *explained* all that. She has been restored to the care of her parents, I believe!"

He looked at Priscilla more closely. She had *seemed* to be listening, but was she just getting more cunning at concealing her inattention?

"*What?*" exclaimed Priscilla, hastily. "*Not* in prison! Elodea should apply immediately for a restraining order or an injunction on the woman! She is clearly *stalking* Elodea! She could be trying to *kill* her again! *Pelle sub agnina latitat mens lupina.*"

"Mama *claims* that Fran is now perfectly safe. Can't get her to say otherwise!" replied Barnabus, wondering if his mama was *really* in any great danger from Fran. Mama being in real danger seemed to him to be like suggesting the cliffs of Dover might disappear suddenly. Mama was always there, always safe. Even though Fran had once kidnapped her and tried to drown her he could not believe that she was anything other than fine now. Nothing had happened when Fran had suddenly materialised in Little Wychwell, and there was no reason to suppose that Fran would ever visit Little Wychwell again. *Was there?* Would Mama have *told* him if that was the case? Suddenly Barnabus felt a chill of fear strike his heart. He was on the verge of leaping out of the door and dashing home to make sure Mama was safe but then he remembered that Dad was working from home today, so Mama would be perfectly well protected. But Barnabus made a mental note to check for sure that Mama had no intention of having any further contact with Fran when he went to see Mama this evening.

He resumed his story. "The *Fran* bit was only *part* of the whole extraordinary sequence of events. I presumed Mama would already have told you about that bit! Bother, the time is *racing* past! This is taking so much longer than I thought because of having to go right back to the Fran bit, and I have to be back in work in half an hour! But wait till you hear what happened to me and Walls!"

"Something happened to you and Walls *as well*? *Malis mala succedunt*!" said Priscilla, in encouraging tones, while arranging her features carefully into the 'attentive and interested' look again.

"I suppose you haven't read the *Oxford Times* recently?" asked Barnabus, without any hope that she had. "No? I'd better explain this next episode from the beginning as well then! And I am sure that this part is somehow connected with Mama meeting Fran, whatever the police think, so listen up carefully. I want your opinion on it! I think we might need to do some *more investigating* together!"

But Priscilla had vanished into her own thoughts very early in the story because Barnabus began with a long monologue about Walls, fortunately before Barnabus reached the point of explaining that Walls needed an occasional lunch break without Yvette. Priscilla and Yvette got on like houses on fire, both being *theoretical* feminists who also both embraced discourse theory, and

Priscilla would have repeated the chauvinist betrayal of Walls to Yvette at the earliest opportunity.

Thus by the time that Barnabus got on to the sighting of the body in the river, Priscilla was wandering in her own happy world. But her subconscious registered a sudden change of inflexion in his voice as he reached the crux of the story, and it metaphorically tapped her on the shoulder and told her to wake up. Having been thus alerted to the fact that something more exciting was about to be revealed, she had resumed listening and happened to catch some rather startling words about how heavy the body had been when they had tried to lift it from the water. These words made her realise she had better pay full attention for a while, as there seemed some danger that Barnabus had turned up to ask her for help in the *disposal* of a large, wet body, and she might agree to this by mistake if she wasn't listening properly. When Barnabus then described his amazement that the body belonged to Ustin and that it had the clear mark of a bullet entering its forehead she felt relieved. Not only had Barnabus and/or Walls, *not* killed the corpse themselves but the identity of the body had not been revealed while she wasn't listening, and she now had sufficient information to be able to actively rejoin the conversation.

"I knew all along that Ustin *wasn't* dead!" Priscilla crowed. "And not just *drowned* but *also shot*! So like Rasputin, *don't you think? Non est ad astra mollis e terris via*!"

She made a resolution to pay full attention to what Barnabus was saying. If *Ustin's body* was involved this account was now becoming genuinely fascinating!

There was then a moment's awkwardness in Barnabus' account when he suddenly remembered he had not mentioned the jogging man who looked so much like Flipper, and absent-mindedly decided to tell Priscilla about the jogger too, in case it was important for their investigation. But then, having nearly let slip Flipper's name, the only route he could think of in order to get himself out of his own self-created dilemma was to describe the jogging man as "a man who looked like someone that Walls and I knew at college but it couldn't be him because he is dead". He had avoided the whole Flipper problem with his mama and Angel by carefully not mentioning the man running along the towpath at all. He shook his head slightly. He must be overtired. How could he have been so stupid?

Possibly he made this error because Priscilla, as an audience, had been everything he had hoped for. She had seemed enraptured with his account. She had *not* told him that he was suffering from stress and imagination when he said that the drowned man was Ustin. When he also told her that he was sure the man was dead before he fell in the river because he had a bullet hole in his forehead, she had seemed *absolutely thrilled*.

The fact the papers had reported the man as being a vagrant and being drowned did not surprise Priscilla at all. She had a low opinion of the care taken by journalists in verifying facts. But the "the man who looked like someone that Walls and I knew at college but it couldn't be him because he is dead" suddenly created an appalling problem for Priscilla herself. Priscilla was quite certain that this could only be one man. It had to be "Flipper of the Blood Diamonds", as she usually labelled him in her own mind. After all, how many people could Walls and Barnabus possibly both know who were supposed to be dead but were actually alive? The fact that Priscilla knew his true identity when she was never officially supposed to have even met Flipper made matters very awkward.

When Barnabus had ended his description of the jogging man she had looked, if Barnabus had been looking at her, decidedly shifty. So when Barnabus paused just after mentioning this man who was supposed to be dead but yet was running up the towpath, Priscilla had no idea how to respond. She could hardly admit that she knew to whom Barnabus was referring. Furthermore, she didn't know if Barnabus himself knew that Flipper was truthfully still alive or whether Barnabus really believed that Flipper was dead. But she didn't like to discuss the matter at all in case she slipped up and broke the Official Secrets Act. She had a horrible vision of the outside gate of a prison in her mind. So she feigned a coughing fit while pondering the matter.

But Priscilla found no quick solution. On consideration it seemed very likely that Barnabus *did* know that Flipper was alive. For if no one else had told him, say someone like Flipper *himself*, then Priscilla was prepared to bet that Walls would have slipped up on this one and accidentally let the truth out to Barnabus. But Priscilla didn't know that *for sure and certain*. Yet if she didn't tackle the subject of the jogger *now*, at once, she might make the mistake of naming the jogger as Flipper in a *later* conversation, and that would be worse. Could Walls and Barnabus possibly have a *collection* of friends who were supposed to be dead and were not? Surely not. Even those two could hardly have more than one such friend. The only possibility was for Priscilla to get Barnabus to accidentally admit that *he* had thought it was Flipper and say the name first, so that she could then use it with impunity herself. But how to achieve this goal? Priscilla needed more time to think. She must gain a longer meditation interval. More coffee; that was it. She would send Barnabus to make more coffee while she thought what to do about this crisis.

"So sorry," she said, as she stopped pretending to cough. She felt she had better stop as the action was making her throat feel quite sore. "Choked on my biscuit! Perhaps more coffee? *Could* you?"

"I suppose so. Yes, I'll get on to it. But I haven't got much time to spare and I haven't even told you the *worst* of this whole affair yet. No one, Aunty Pris, *no one* except you will *believe* me. They all think I imagined the whole Ustin thing due to stress, and that it was just a local down-and-out that I thought was Ustin! *So*," he said, putting heavy emphasis on this concluding moment, as he finally finished his gigantic narrative, "that's the whole story! What do *you* think?"

"*I* think I *need more coffee*!" she said. "Go and make us another jugful! *Cogito summere potum alterum*! You could find a bottle of wine and some glasses if you don't have time to make the coffee!"

Barnabus ignored her final sentence but still sighed slightly as he headed for the kitchen with the tray. He knew where everything was in Priscilla's kitchen, as Angel had boarded with her for many years, but he still wished that Priscilla did not have the impression that younger visitors to her house could be used as substitutes for the college staff. When Priscilla was in Coromandel College she never had to make her own coffee as it was provided in the Senior Common Room or the Hall, and she took most of her meals at High Table and never cooked. Barnabus was hungry despite eating most of a plate of biscuits. He had missed his lunch to call round here. He looked hopefully in the fridge but Priscilla didn't have any food in it at all. Why hadn't he bought sandwiches and brought them with him? All he could find by way of nourishment was some more biscuits lurking at the back of one of the kitchen cupboards. He didn't really want *more* biscuits but he added a plate of them to the coffee. One must forage for what one could find where one could.

By the time he returned to the lounge Priscilla had remembered that she *did* officially know that Flipper was supposed to be *dead* even though she had never officially met him. Furthermore, she could not recall any of Barnabus' other university friends having died, although she could have missed this fact. Since she knew that Flipper was supposed to be dead, and had, indeed, discussed the funeral with Barnabus, she could simply ask him if it had been Flipper that Barnabus thought he had seen. Then he would have to admit that it was! So she was sitting bolt upright and alert, looking very self-satisfied and wearing a smug grin, when the coffee arrived.

"Tell me!" she said, quickly, before he began a different conversational gambit and distracted her.

"Yes?" he said, glad to find someone who was interested enough in the story to want amplification of the fine details.

"Was it *Flipper* that you thought you saw jogging past?" she asked.

Barnabus was now nonplussed. How had she guessed that? Had he somehow, by mistake, managed to let Angel know that Flipper was alive? If he had then Angel might have told Priscilla. But Angel always seemed to genuinely believe that Flipper was dead, and he had not told Angel about the jogger at all! He had not told Mama either. Could *Walls* have told Priscilla that Flipper was alive? But why would Walls do that? It wasn't likely. Why had he gone and told Priscilla about the jogger being someone they thought was dead? What an idiot he was!

Then the same thought struck Barnabus that had previously struck Priscilla. He chastised himself! Of course she had just guessed that the only one of his friends that she knew was dead must be the one who had appeared jogging down the towpath.

"No, no! It was *another* friend!" he said hastily. "But it *can't* have been Flipper because he's dead!"

"Two of your friends have died since you left Kings!" said Priscilla. "*Two* of them! At your age! It scarcely seems possible!"

Since she did not believe this in the slightest she added, in a very melodramatic way, "*Quam cito transit gloria mundi.*"

"Absolutely! All that education and effort for nothing, what?" said Barnabus, to fill in time while he thought on his feet and came up with a plausible cause of death. "Mountaineering accident! Lots of mountaineering enthusiasts at Kings. Used to do a bit myself!" said Barnabus, inventing on his feet. "Mountaineering definitely lowers life expectancy. Poor Flavian: fell down a crevasse on a glacier. Very sad! We were all really cut up at the time! Obviously it wasn't him. Quite impossible, with him being definitely dead. It must have been someone who just looked like him! I just told you that we both thought that to show you how much we were both in a state of shock – me because of the drowned man being Ustin, and Walls because he was totally freaked about having to pick up a dead body. *That* was absolutely not the important bit of the story. I can't even think why I mentioned it! The *important* bit is that the body *was* Ustin and the police are claiming it wasn't, and he *was* shot and not drowned, and nobody will believe me about either of those facts! And even Mama, *even Mama*, says I was clearly overstressed and must have imagined them."

Barnabus hoped he could remember the name Flavian for future reference. What a ridiculous name to choose! He should have said something easy to remember like *James*. Not just easier to remember, but there must have been dozens of Jameses at Kings when he was there, whereas he was not at all sure that there was anyone called Flavian in the place at the same time as himself. He would have to check the year name lists and find out if there was and, if so, discover some more details on the man, for surely one Flavian was the most you could expect. It would be just like Priscilla to check the university and college lists herself and catch him out!

This would not do at all, thought Priscilla. She had wanted Barnabus to admit that he thought the man was Flipper to guard against later slips of her own tongue. She sat in silence, glaring at him. Then she had another good idea on how to prevent Barnabus from making her slip up about Flipper if she investigated this matter any further with him. She would simply stop him from further detective work at all. She made a triumphant pronouncement, "I see why everyone else tells you that you made a mistake about Ustin. They are trying to stop you from continuing to poke round in this case. You *should* be able to see why you *mustn't* investigate further!"

"*What*?" asked Barnabus, enormously disappointed at her taking the other side.

"Well, isn't it obvious? Your friend who was supposed to be dead is still alive, and you *saw* him. And Ustin, who was presumed dead years ago, was also really alive before he was really dead, and then the police pretend Ustin was someone else. There's only one conclusion and… Can't you *see*? They must *all be secret agents*! Only from different sides! Ustin must be an agent for whichever country he really comes from, and your friend

– wotsisname – he must be a British secret agent! You were just *told* that he blew up, er, I mean blew *off*, er, I mean *fell* off a mountain or whatever you said. That's why you must not investigate further. It's too dangerous! *Quod erat demonstrandum*. You don't want to get *mixed up with secret agents*! I *quiver* at the thought of it myself!" she announced. "In fact, if I met a real secret agent I think I would die of fright."

'Quivering at the thought of it' was quite true, she thought to herself, even if the 'dying of fright' bit was not. For on the occasion on which she had met some secret agents, including Flipper, they had appeared to be more eccentric than your average Oxford academic. Enough to make anyone quiver but with suppressed laughter and not with fright! Even at the memory of the encounter she had to stifle a giggle.

Barnabus was not paying any attention to her. He was sitting, coffee poised halfway to his mouth and looking dumbstruck. Priscilla did not notice his suspended animation, being fully occupied with her own thoughts.

Barnabus finally pulled himself together, raised the cup to his lips and drank the coffee. He looked at the clock. He stood up.

"So, you aren't interested in helping me find out the truth either. I must get back to work!" he said, rather tight-lipped. "I apologise for wasting your time, Aunty Pris!"

He looked as though she had slapped him in the face. He had thought that Priscilla, of all people, would have taken an interest in *investigating* this conundrum *further*. Priscilla looked at his face and felt truly sorry. She should have been more sympathetic. She felt annoyed with herself too as she would have *loved* to investigate this matter with him, and now she had slammed the door in her own face! Stupid Flipper! Stupid people who pretend to be dead when they are alive and then won't let you say they are alive! Stupid, stupid secret agents and governments and Official Secrets Acts and prevaricators and…

"You *didn't* waste my time!" she cried. "I *love* to see you, Barnabus; you know that! I love to see you *any time*! Come *again*! *Soon*! And, and, take another biscuit with you! To eat on the way back! *You haven't had any lunch*!"

She picked a biscuit up from the plate and waved it in front of his face. He looked at the biscuit, and then at her, still with a bemused expression. He was so shocked at this betrayal, by her! He had been *sure* she would have supported his ideas about investigating further together. From the vague way he looked at the biscuit an impartial observer might have concluded that he had never seen a biscuit before and had no idea what it was.

"Look!" said Priscilla, helpfully, in the coaxing tone of voice that owners might use when trying to entice a small growling dog out from under a chair. "*Biscuit*! No, not *one* biscuit! *The whole plateful*! Look! *Chocolate* biscuits! You'll be hungry this afternoon otherwise! *Sum ergo edo*!"

The coaxing tone seemed to work. Barnabus finally focussed on the biscuits and recovered his usual poise and elegance. He even forgave her. She was trying to keep him *safe*, he supposed. Rather *sweet* really. Bless the old girl! She had managed to climb down from the heady heights of academic thoughts to the lower levels of reality and realise that he had an empty stomach. Barnabus gathered up *all* the biscuits from the plate.

"Thank you, Aunty Pris! Look at the time! Must fly!" he said, and bent to kiss her on the cheek as he hurried out, clutching the large pile of biscuits between his hands. He managed to balance his biscuit hoard successfully on one palm as he let himself out through the door. His departure was so sudden that Priscilla remained sitting in the lounge, calling "Goodbye!" to his retreating back. Fortunately she had no idea that he had just classified her as "old girl".

Barnabus sighed as he jogged back to work – an unwise procedure with a mouth full of biscuit crumbs which then sprayed everywhere. He paused to brush them from his jacket and shirt. But it was a happy sigh, for as he had cantered back to the centre he had thought about the strange reactions everyone kept giving him. Now at last he understood why they were all apparently refusing to believe him. It wasn't because they *disbelieved* him about Ustin; they were just worried about his safety if he started poking about in this particular mystery! Even those who did not know about the jogger could see that his account of a man in the river who he thought was a notorious criminal, come back to life and then shot but who the police said wasn't the said criminal and hadn't been shot, did suggest a most dangerous intrigue. He could see this now. It was truthfully very kind of them all but very inconvenient when he wanted a partner in crime investigation! He opened the door to the suite of offices where he worked, paused, straightened up and squared his shoulders. He marched forward to his desk with the certain determination that if no one else would help him he would just investigate this one all on his own and find out the whole truth for himself.

Chapter 5

As Barnabus sat down at his desk and started work he felt self-satisfied and pleased with his decision to go solo. If he had been able to see the worried emails that had passed between Elodea and Walls on the previous evening he would have stopped feeling pleased and would feel agitated and annoyed. For the two of them were wondering what they could do about the fact that Barnabus was so overtired by doing his job and looking after his two small children that he had not only imagined that a random homeless man was Ustin, but also that the man had been shot and not drowned.

However, this email exchange had happened yesterday, whereas if Barnabus could have seen inside the Old Vicarage *at that very* moment, he would have felt much *more* pleased than he did right now, not only with how right his own opinions were now, but how right they always had been.

For Elodea had a nighttime wildlife camera, which she set up occasionally in an effort to see what ran around in the garden when she was asleep. But whenever she put the camera out the wildlife seemed to be wise to her intentions. No matter how many droppings and tracks they *usually* left in her garden overnight – very sure evidence of their presence there – they *never* materialised in front of the camera lens. Elodea imagined them all shushing and pointing and then tiptoeing around the back of it, despite the manufacturer's assurances of its unobtrusive nature.

So Elodea had devised a plan to outwit them. She had hidden the camera in the front hedge so it was looking at the road rather than into the garden. For surely, she reasoned, the wildlife would not evade the camera by going round the back of it once she had done that because avoiding it would now require the effort of pushing in and out of a hedge. Pleased with this piece of butchered logic, she had thus set the camera up last night, cunningly concealed among the twigs and leaves but with a good view of the road, as soon as she had returned from Pippy's final 10.00 p.m. walk.

It wasn't a choir practice night so, except for the Vicar, no one would be likely to be walking along past her house between then and her removing the camera at 6.00 a.m. when she took Pippy out for her first trot around the garden. Thus she told herself that she need not feel guilty about intruding on other people's privacy. The Vicar would not mind the camera being there even if he knew; she was sure of that. He was so keen on wildlife himself he would entirely understand her interest in its behaviour.

First thing that morning she had switched the camera off and taken it back into the house but had not yet had leisure to look and see if she had any photographs.

She could have looked at it earlier but she was also enjoying having a little break from Amadeus and Theodora, not so she could do something else but so she did not have to do anything in particular. Thus she had spent a lot of the morning lounging on one of the collapsing sofas in the lounge, suspended neatly between the broken springs, Pippy asleep on her stomach. Elodea was supposedly reading a book, but her eyes were closed and her breathing was very regular and gentle.

After this exhausting morning she had lunched on a large piece of cake and a mug of coffee and then remembered that she had not yet investigated the contents of the camera. She felt the usual frisson of excitement as she extracted the memory card from the camera and plugged it into her computer. What would she find? Deer? Rabbits? Foxes? Badgers? She *must* have captured something gambolling in the lane. At least one rabbit or one fox, surely? She was doomed to disappointment. There was just a succession of blank shots. Could they possibly have realised the camera was there and sprinted past it too fast for the shutter? Then, at last, an image! No, it was only the Vicar, grey and slightly blurred but definitely the Vicar: you could see his birdwatching binoculars swinging. He was presumably going along to the churchyard to study the owls, or possibly the bats. Then more blank shots. The rest were almost bound to be birds flitting around after sunrise. But no, here was someone else: the shadowy figure of another person. It was not the Vicar this time. It was someone who tiptoed furtively past the camera and then positioned themselves a little further down, sitting in the hedge, opposite Elodea's front gate. Presumably the unknown person readjusted their position from time to time for there were some more intermittent shots of a figure among the hedge. Then the storage on the card must have filled up for the photographs stopped abruptly just after 3.00 a.m.

Elodea had no doubt who this figure must be. It was impossible not to recognise her. It was Fran. Elodea screamed involuntarily. She nearly dashed outside right away to check whether Fran was still there. But then she chided herself for stupidity. If Fran had still been there then Elodea would have seen her when she collected the camera.

Elodea restudied the photos. They were very low resolution and rather blurred. Maybe she was wrong? Perhaps it was someone else? No, for Fran's face was quite clear in one or two of them. It *was* Fran. It had to be. She seemed to be wearing her 'tramp' clothes again but the face was Fran's. Not a shadow of a doubt.

Elodea hunted through her memory for any possible *good* reason for Fran's presence. For a minute or so she tried to convince herself that Fran believed that Ustin was around in the area again, and that Fran was guarding Elodea in case Ustin attacked her. But Elodea knew with a dull, sad certainty, entirely based on illogical telepathy, that this was not the case. Fran had seen the tramp who had then drowned walking along the towpath, and thought he was Ustin. He must look similar to Ustin, for Barnabus had made the same mistake. But Fran must have then regressed to her jealous conviction that Ustin was in love with Elodea. Fran must now be stalking Elodea, hoping to catch her out. She had decided to *actually* kill Elodea this time. Elodea, with all her belief in the innate goodness of everyone, with all her readiness to forgive and forget at all times, suddenly relived the moments of fear when Fran had trapped her in a boat on the cold and fast-flowing Cherwell, and shivered.

Elodea could not discuss this matter with Barnabus, who was already overwrought about his own supposed sighting of Ustin. She could not discuss it with John as he got very worked up and completely out of sorts every time she and Barnabus became accidentally tangled up in criminal events, as if they had done it on purpose. There was only one person she could talk to. Elodea snatched the little card from the computer, grabbed Pippy, leapt out of the house and rushed towards her car. She paused for a moment and checked all around the vehicle, underneath it and inside it, lest Fran had somehow concealed herself there. Then she threw Pippy into the passenger seat, got into the driver's seat, locked herself in lest Fran was hovering at the next road junction to spring into the car with her, and headed for Oxford.

* * *

Priscilla, hearing the doorbell give that prolonged and repeated 'Smith Family' ring for the second time in one day, jumped in her chair again, but much more violently than last time. She sank back onto the seat, trembling slightly. Not *another* Smith visitation? Just when she was making such good progress! Then she realised that Barnabus must have left something in the house. She would just pop down, let him collect whatever it was and then come back. But she pressed 'save' on her edits before heading towards the door. You could never tell how long being vulcanised by a Smith family member might take, even if they did claim to only be popping in and out.

"Hello! What did you leave…?" Priscilla said before she even had the door fully open.

But to Priscilla's amazement it was not Barnabus, it was Elodea.

Elodea had now worked herself up into a complete panic. She had kept checking the mirror all the way to Oxford to make sure that Fran was not driving the car immediately behind hers, and even taken a few surprising diversions on her route to make absolutely sure that she was not being followed by any of the cars that she could see in her rear view mirror.

While Priscilla was still suspended, mid-sentence, due to surprise at her caller's identity, Elodea, anticipating the final word, cried, "I left *nothing* here, *nothing*!" pushed past her friend into the hall, wrenched the door from Priscilla and slammed it shut.

Then Elodea leant against the wall, breathing hard, recovering from all her imagined dangers.

"Elodea! Good afternoon! How lovely to see you! Coffee?" said Priscilla, calmly. "I mean, may I *offer* you coffee? Or would you like to go out to a café and partake of some there?"

"Certainly," said Elodea, between gasps. "I would love a cup of coffee. Thank you so much, Priscilla. But, if you don't mind, I would prefer if we could take coffee in your house today, rather than going to a café."

"Enchanted!" replied Priscilla. "I will go and make some. Do go into the lounge and make yourself comfortable."

"I entirely forgot myself, Priscilla," said Elodea, pulling herself up, and adopting a more formal tone. "How *very* rude of me! How lovely to see you, too! How are you?"

"I am very well, thank you," replied Priscilla. "And yourself?"

"Yes, very well also," said Elodea.

Thus social conventions and polite behaviour demonstrated their skills at overcoming the awkwardness inherent in a fugitive friend arriving unexpectedly inside one's house.

"And how is *Charles*?" continued Elodea, who having begun appropriate social conversation found herself entirely unable to stop.

"Astonishingly well when I last saw him" replied Priscilla, "In fact quite incredible for his age. There are those who say he should be forced to resign the Chair so it can be awarded to someone less *senile*, I mean to say, someone not *quite so venerable* but I *personally* feel his academic grasp is still *perfectly sound*."

Elodea was entirely floored by this reply. She took a deep breath and considered what it could possibly mean. She rapidly concluded that Priscilla was not referring to her husband Charles but to a Professor at Coromandel College where Priscilla herself worked. Priscilla's husband Charles *was* a Professor but in a Canadian university and Priscilla could not possibly be referring to her husband as incredible *for his age* since he was the same age as Priscilla and Elodea themselves.

"No, no, I meant how is *Charles*, as in your *husband* Charles" Elodea corrected gently.

"Oh, *Charles*!" Priscilla trilled a pretend laugh, shrilly, to show she didn't mind her own little mistake, "Naturally! You meant *Charles*! He was very well when I spoke to him last, I mean when we spoke *yesterday*, obviously we talk to each other *every* day, yes, yes, *very* well!"

Elodea wondered how long ago Priscilla and Charles had actually last spoken, in their cases it could have been several months ago, and yet they seemed to remain steadfastly and even happily married.

"That reminds me! Charles had a *message* for *you* which I have not yet passed on" Priscilla suddenly recalled, "mea culpa. Although it is the *first* time I have seen you since *yesterday* so I could hardly have passed it on any earlier. Something to do with a *cinema*, wait just a moment while I recall the *exact* words."

"A *cinema*?" asked Elodea, now very puzzled.

"Yes, a cinema, up a *mountain*" said Priscilla, impressing herself with her own powers of recall of totally unimportant non- academic facts, "He ran into a cinema which you knew well."

"Er, where is he at present?" asked Elodea, wondering if she had acquaintance with *any* cinemas any more as she was quite unable to remember the last time she had visited one to watch a film. She went to the Little Wychwell Film Club in the Village Hall occasionally but

Charles could hardly have been in Little Wychwell without Elodea knowing about it, someone in the village would certainly have told her about the stranger in their midst.

"In Nepal, on an *expedition*, tackling a new *route*" lied Priscilla, hoping that Elodea would not ask her for further details, as, in truth, she had no idea where Charles had been when he last rang, not even which country he had been in, almost certainly he had been up a mountain since that was where he spent most of his free time. At this *precise* moment Priscilla thought, on consideration, that it was quite probable that he was in his laboratory in Canada.

Fortunately Elodea accepted Priscilla's answer without question because she was so intrigued by the cinema aspect.

"But I have never been to Nepal" Elodea replied "And certainly not to a cinema!"

"Maybe Little Wychwell church raised money to build a cinema there" suggested Priscilla, "For the education and entertainment of the indigenous people."

"Perfectly *possible*" said Elodea, "Although I can't remember us doing so. Perhaps Charles meant to say *Barnabus* and not me, maybe Barnabus and his friends built a cinema there in their gap year?"

"*Coul*d be" agreed Priscilla, vaguely, for she had lost all interest in the subject some time ago. She wished she had never mentioned it at all. She had passed the message onwards, surely that was sufficient? One would think Elodea might be more *grateful* and less *argumentative*.

Then Elodea giggled.

"Something *funny* that I *missed*?" asked Priscilla, in her severest 'not amused tutor to student' tone.

"No" said Elodea, but having to suppress another giggle before continuing, "You are so right, we *did* send money to build a cinema in Nepal. How could I have forgotten? I was just remembering something funny that happened when we were fund raising for it. Too complicated to explain, it involved, er, the Vicar and Lady Wilmington and a *pig*. Thank you for letting me know that the cinema is still there. The Vicar will be *so* pleased to hear that it's being used."

Elodea uncrossed her fingers, which she had crossed to avert the shocking string of lies that she had just told.

For Elodea had finally untangled the twisted message by reversing Priscilla's word association, cinema, film, flick, Flic, Tony and Flic. Clearly Charles must have met Elodea's oldest son Tony and his wife Flic who were on Buddhist Pilgrimage in the Himalayas. She had wondered for a moment whether to attempt to explain this to Priscilla but had decided to take the simpler and faster path of untruth. "Forgive me, Lord, I don't want to upset Priscilla further by explaining this one" she prayed, silently.

"The coffee!" Priscilla pronounced, "I must make some! *Tempus fugit*!"

Priscilla turned towards the kitchen and then looked back towards her friend. "One moment!" she said "Is there *imminent* danger?"

"Indeed, no! At least, I don't *believe* so," replied Elodea, with guilty honesty. "It is *entirely* possible that the danger may, in fact, be *completely imaginary*."

"Good," said Priscilla.

"Quite so," said Elodea. "Are you sure you don't need help with the coffee?"

"No, thank you," replied Priscilla. "Do go and sit down. You seem a little, er, *exhausted*."

Elodea went obediently into the lounge and sat down, thinking how wonderful it must be to have such a neat and tidy house, even though she also reflected that this was due to Priscilla not having men, dogs and children barging untidily all over it.

Priscilla trotted off to the kitchen, pausing briefly to put the security chain on the front door. One never knew what might happen once one had a *Smith* in the house, even one who believed the danger to be *imaginary*. She eyed the heavy hall chair. Perhaps she should put that in front of the door as well? No, Elodea *had* said *completely imaginary*, had she not? She went past the chair to the kitchen but then reversed, heaved the chair across the hall and wedged it against the front door. There!

Soon they were both perched on Priscilla's brand-new low leather white sofa in front of her elegant new Italian coffee table which was now bearing the delicate bone china coffee utensils. Elodea looked with envy at the sofa, the table, the cups and the brand-new *white* lounge carpet, a *white* carpet of the *thickest* pile. Living alone had compensations! Elodea sighed as she thought what this carpet would look like if it was laid down in her lounge for, say, half an hour. Then she thought of all the very much-loved people that she lived with and decided she would much rather have them than the carpet. But it *would* be pleasant to have a sofa whose springs were still completely hidden by its upholstery. Maybe not in white, though. Dark brown with black and grey specks perhaps?

While Elodea indulged in this civilised interior design daydream Priscilla was looking with alarm at the state of Elodea's clothes, hair and trainers. Elodea had deposited a trail of pine needles and other pieces of small debris across the new carpet. Priscilla was wondering if Elodea had *finished* 'shedding' now, or whether she was going to continue to deposit detritus over the house for her entire visit. At least, she thought, Elodea had *not* brought her monstrously behaved, if tiny and cute, dog with her. But just as Priscilla lifted her coffee to take the first sip, she was interrupted by a squawk from Elodea.

"*Pippy*!" Elodea cried. "You don't think she will be getting *too hot* in the car? I didn't bring her in when I first arrived because she was fast asleep and she looked so peaceful. She's *getting on a bit*, you know. I left all the windows part open but it might still be getting really hot. Also I shouldn't have left her out there because of the probably imagined danger. What was I thinking of? Anything could happen!"

"No!" replied Priscilla, firmly, and, feeling truly impressed with her own inspiration, continued, "I would think that today's temperature is not at all excessive. And if the danger is imaginary there is no reason to suppose she is not perfectly safe. Also, if the danger is not imaginary but is somehow *attached to you*, as I deduce from your behaviour, then she is almost certainly safer out there."

"If you are *sure* about that I *suppose* she will be fine. But are you very busy, Priscilla?" Elodea continued, remembering her manners again. "I do hope I am not interrupting your studies?"

"It's OK. You were not interrupting anything of great import to the world," said Priscilla. "I don't have any *time* to do *proper study* at the minute. *Pendent opera interrupta!*"

"You don't have any *time*?" responded Elodea, wondering in alarm if her friend was ill with a terrible disease and spending all her time in hospital outpatients appointments. This was the only explanation she could conjure up as to why Priscilla might not be currently engaged in her usual deep academic study. Elodea restrained a smile at the idea that Priscilla's study might usually be of any import to the world in general and then demanded, "*Why* don't you have enough time?"

"It's our new Glorious Leader, the Prevaricator of Coromandel," wailed Priscilla. "He has insisted that I produce a report on 'The Relevance of Classical Studies to the World of Modern Business and Economics' by the end of the month. All the faculties in the college have to produce one on their own subject to justify their existence."

"But," said Elodea, "having to write such a report is quite ridiculous!"

Fortunately Priscilla interrupted her *before* Elodea could add the thoughtless words: "Classical Studies don't need to have any relevance to the world of modern business and economics. They aren't *supposed* to have any!"

"*Absolutely!*" Priscilla exclaimed. "And that is what I told the Prevaricator at the time. It is absolutely unnecessary to explain the use of Classical Studies because these studies are the basis of the whole of modern business life and industry. That should be obvious even to the most uneducated and ignorant, even to those whose original degree was in *Economics*, which is *quite* clearly of no use to *anyone* whatsoever. *Post hoc ergo propter hoc*!"

"So your new prevaricator read Economics?" asked Elodea.

"He read PPE originally, but Economics is his *main* specialisation, yes, and then he has the *nerve* to ask *me* to justify the existence of *Classics*!" expostulated Priscilla.

"I absolutely agree," said Elodea. "Economics is a *complete* waste of time! *Absolutely* useless in almost every way!"

Elodea felt qualified to pronounce on this, for she had read PPE herself.

Priscilla launched into an exasperated speech. "It is not difficult to justify the use of Classical Studies, obviously. I send the Prevaricator an extra chapter of my report *every day*. By the end of the month he cannot *possibly* be unaware of the relevance that Classics have to *every* aspect of business and industry. I have, so far, covered civil and military engineering, transport systems, sewage and water systems, plumbing and heating, and the application of the Roman knowledge base to current applications. I am currently engaged in a special case study on concrete and building on marshy foundations in connection with the Pantheon. I will move on from this useful case study, which makes a link between engineering and architecture, to the influence of the Romans on modern architecture, and then I will continue through medicine, military strategy and diplomacy, education and government. I feel that will be quite sufficient for the *Ancient Roman* angle although it will still only cover a small subset of the entire subject. I could write about such things for eternity and never finish. But I must move on after that and scamper briefly through the Ancient Greek material: geometry, more architecture, physics, astronomy, government and so on and so on. But this is such a waste of my time! Having to sit and type such *trivia* is wrecking my research. *Piscem nature docem*!"

"I can see that it must be trying," said Elodea, thinking that quite possibly the Prevaricator of Coromandel College, where Priscilla was a don, might be regretting his decision to ask Priscilla to produce such information in the first place, especially since she would probably cross-examine him to make sure he had read and absorbed every syllable next time she saw him. Even worse, he had asked every don in his college to produce a similar report. A small smile curved around the edges of Elodea's mouth as she envisaged the results of his request: thousands and thousands of words being typed by a set of enraged and defiant dons, all of whom sincerely and fervently believed that the whole world revolved around their own specialism.

Then a dreadful thought struck Elodea. She did not want her friend to lose her job because the Prevaricator could not read her reports. She decided to put it as tactfully as she could.

"Priscilla, you are, you *are* writing these reports in *English*, aren't you?" she asked, nervously.

"I *have* to do so, *apparently*. The man can't read a word of Latin! Or Greek! *Not one word*! And he is the *Prevaricator of Coromandel College*! What is the world coming to? No wonder British business and economics is in a mess when economists haven't even studied Classics! Never! Not at all! He sent my first report back to me and demanded that I *translate* it *before he would read it*!"

"*Astonishing!*" breathed Elodea, hoping the sentiment sounded convincing.

"Although," Priscilla said, in a tone that would have frightened any student within range, "he can, apparently, use Wikipedia; he had the utter nerve to put *quidquid Latine dictum sit altum videtur* at the end of his remarks."

Elodea was genuinely shocked by this boorish behaviour. "Priscilla," she exclaimed, "how perfectly, perfectly appalling. The man has *no manners*! Perhaps the

Classics are his *Pons Asinorum*?" Then she giggled, and added, "You should have written back: '*retine vim istam falsa enim dicam si coges*'!"

"Quite so. *Risum tenatis, amici*?" said Priscilla, now entirely satisfied with Elodea's reaction to her tale of woe and able to move on to discovering the reason for Elodea's unexpected appearance in her house, "But that's enough about *me*! *Do* tell me. I am all *agog*. What danger have you imagined yourself to be in?"

Priscilla was quite certain that the danger was indeed non-existent, for she knew that Elodea suffered from massive excesses of imagination. Thus she could sit back and listen without any worry about actual peril that was likely to arrive in her own house in pursuit of Elodea. But Priscilla was, nonetheless, feeling anxious. For she needed to prevent herself from making the faux pas of mentioning that she had already been visited by Barnabus that morning, or of letting slip any information that Barnabus had just told her when she commented on whatever story Elodea was about to recount. For Elodea would undoubtedly notice any little errors of this nature. Priscilla felt very proud of herself because she had realised that Barnabus might not want Elodea to know of his determination to continue investigating the 'Drowned Ustin' case or that he had been at her house. Elodea's 'danger' was almost certainly connected with Fran's reappearance in her life, so this should mean that Elodea was going to tell her an almost identical story to

Barnabus. So all she had to do was listen to the entire narrative in silence and her problems about letting the cat out of the bag would be over.

"It's a *very* long story," said Elodea, "and I feel really *guilty* now, Priscilla, because I haven't told you *anything* about *any* of the events which have led up to this *crisis*! We can't have talked for far longer than I had thought. I'm sort of busy with the infants these days, you know. Time runs on. I hardly know where to begin the story! It's all so dreadfully complicated! Barnabus finding another body. Fran, and Ustin and… Well, really, I don't know where to start to explain it all!"

"My, my! What *has* been going on?" said Priscilla, hoping this sounded truthful and adding, apparently carelessly, a line of song, to cover her own fib, "Start at the very beginning. It's a very good place to start!"

Even this sally failed to raise a smile from Elodea, who was taking the consideration of how best to order her long and involved narrative very seriously.

"I think I'd better start with me taking Amadeus to nursery on that fateful day," Elodea decided.

Priscilla groaned inwardly. She might have known that some of Elodea's *so tedious* grandchildren were bound to get major roles in this story. But she had a lucky solution to this problem. She could take a gamble on Barnabus' account being *almost identical* to Elodea's, which meant that she did not need to listen to a single word that her friend was saying. Accordingly she settled her face into 'polite and attentive' and wandered away to a better and more interesting place.

Elodea's voice squeaked on and on and on and on. Finally she stopped.

Priscilla had sagged comfortably into the sofa during the monologue but her subconscious noticed the absence of sound, and bounced her into a more rigid pose with a start. She was ready to launch her plan. All she had to do now was to get Elodea to repeat the part of her account that Barnabus could not have covered, namely whatever had driven Elodea from her own house and made her dash so precipitately to Priscilla's this morning. Clearly this information must have been in the *final* section of her account.

"Elodea, dear," Priscilla said, humbly, "you know what I'm like. I was right there with you for most of your wonderful story and then I *slightly* lost track of that very *last* bit. Could you just run over *who* it was you thought might be *pursuing* you to my *door* again."

Elodea glared at her. She *knew* Priscilla hadn't been listening. She had known it all along! All these years of talking at Priscilla while Priscilla never listened to a word she said. Yet even Elodea had been fooled by her this time, for Priscilla had *looked* as if she was listening! Elodea had checked her face every now and then. The woman must have been taking acting classes. Surely she hadn't stopped listening *near the beginning*, had she?

"*Where* exactly did you stop listening?" Elodea asked.

"After the discovery of a body by Barnabus and Walls that seemed to be Ustin's, and the man running along the towpath who looked like Flipper, and Fran visiting you and then running along the A34 and being stopped by the police," said Priscilla, very glibly.

"What man running along the towpath who looked like Flipper? I didn't say anything about any man who looked like Flipper!" said Elodea.

"Ah, I must have invented that bit!" lied Priscilla. "Er, maybe *that* was where I lost attention, *when they found the body*? I must have wandered off and put Flipper in myself for some odd reason. Maybe I had actually dozed off rather than daydreaming? Bit of a heavy lunch!"

"*Have you been talking to Barnabus recently*?" demanded Elodea, with a sudden rush of extrasensory perception. Priscilla could only have got that information by talking to Barnabus! Obviously! Barnabus had talked to his mama. He had talked to Walls. They had told him he was imagining things. Naturally the next place he would look for sympathy would be *Priscilla*! But why had Barnabus never mentioned a man on the towpath who looked like Flipper to his own *mama*, and yet told *Priscilla* about it? That was odd.

"No, *not at all*. Not for *months*!" said Priscilla. "He's so busy working, and now that Angel lives with him and not with me, well, I hardly see the boy!"

"Hmmmph!" said Elodea, sceptically, thinking she must ask Barnabus about the man on the towpath who looked like Flipper the very next time she saw him. But for now she decided to ignore the perfidy of her friend and assume that Priscilla had got the basic gist of the *prequel* to today's events from Barnabus. In any case the part of the story that Elodea particularly wanted Priscilla to grasp was the *final* part, so she omitted to repeat the events prior to that and began her tale again from the section labelled in her mind as "Events Concerning the Camera in the Hedge".

This time Priscilla made an enormous effort to force herself to remain attentive. She absolutely must not risk further slip-ups. She decided to translate everything that Elodea was saying into Ancient Greek in order to keep her mind on the subject. Her reactions at the end proved the efficacy of this method. Her concentration had, indeed, been perfect.

"*Fran*!" exclaimed Priscilla, who was both impressed and amazed by this revelation. "*In the hedge*! *Outside your house*! How many times, Elodea, *how many times* do I have to tell you that that woman is *dangerous* and you should keep *right out of her way*? Thank goodness I put the chain on the door after you came in! She might have broken in here otherwise! *Ut Roma cadit sic omnis terra.*"

"*So,*" said Elodea, who had decided to ignore with dignity the implications that it was *her own fault* that Fran had reappeared in her life or that Priscilla's house was in some way the centre of the modern universe, "*what do we do next?*"

"I think we should re-examine those photos first. I suppose you didn't think of sending me an email with a copy of them attached?" asked Priscilla.

"I didn't need to!" replied Elodea, feeling technologically brilliant. "Because I brought the little camera card thingy with me! I had the sense to seize it from my computer just before I left the house!"

"In that case I had better repair upstairs to my office and look at them immediately!" said Priscilla, glad to find that Elodea was meekly letting her take command and not vying for the top position, as Barnabus would have done.

"I'll come too. Then I can explain the photos!" said Elodea.

Priscilla looked at Elodea. Could she persuade Elodea to sit still in the lounge while only Priscilla went upstairs, or should she just resign herself to allowing Elodea to pollute the upper echelons of the house with whatever objects she had stuck to her clothes, hair and footwear?

Priscilla remembered that her cleaning lady was due in tomorrow and resigned herself to the temporary disaster. She looked harder at Elodea and sighed as she realised the precise nature of what she had previously thought was some sort of intentional hair ornament.

"Elodea, dear, I can't *imagine* how they got there but you seem to have several twigs tangled in your hair!" she said.

"Oh, yes!" said Elodea, perfectly calm and not making any sign of being about to remove them. "The *hedge*, you see! First thing this morning. I had to reach through it to get to the camera! I haven't looked in the mirror since!"

"Ah!" said Priscilla, thinking that this at least in part explained the trail of vegetation that was being left by Elodea. "Up we go then!"

If Priscilla had seen inside Elodea's car she would have realised that significant quantities of vegetation had also been acquired from its seats and floor because Elodea had a habit of parking the vehicle beneath the trees and forgetting to wind her windows back up.

Despite her spoken suggestion of motion, Priscilla remained stationary. She was pondering on *how* to get off her so *very* beautiful but armless and extremely low sofa. The sofa was so very new that Barnabus had been her first visitor since its installation and she had managed not to attempt to rise during his visit, remaining seated till after he had left. Priscilla was prepared to suffer for the cause of art and exquisite design and, on discovering that it was impossible for her to rise from her brand-new sofa in a dignified manner, she had devised a method of throwing herself sideways and forwards onto her stomach along the sofa, then rolling off, landing on her knees on the carpet and finally rising from there with the aid of the coffee table. She had now accomplished this often enough for her to be able to complete the manoeuvre quite snappily. But she could hardly take this approach *in front of anyone else*, let alone the irritatingly supple Elodea. But Elodea *was* the same age as herself. Perhaps she was not *so* supple any more either? Priscilla decided to wait and see how her friend tackled the problem of rising *first*, and then perhaps they could help each other up and laugh about it? But Elodea, accustomed to prising herself out of the Old Vicarage's sofa's collapsing springs and webbing and also being several stones lighter and more in the habit of taking regular exercise, bounced straight up onto her feet without pausing to think. The woman, thought Priscilla, was *completely unbearable*!

"Do *go ahead*. I'll *follow*! *Festina lente*!" cooed Priscilla.

Obediently Elodea left the room without questioning why she needed to make haste if Priscilla did not. Priscilla made a mental note to spend a few hours discovering and practising more dignified methods of extracting herself from her own sofa in the hope of finding one that she could use in public. She then applied her rolling and kneeling method and dashed after her friend, panting up the stairs so fast that she was only one step behind Elodea by the time they reached the landing.

Priscilla hastily closed the Pantheon case study on her computer before Elodea could have any opportunity to damage it. Then, slowly and with irritating thoroughness, Priscilla closed all her other open windows just in case of accident. They did not have anything secret or valuable in them but one never knew what might happen with Smiths in the house. Finally Priscilla inserted the little camera memory card in the reader, maddeningly slowly, while Elodea, who was standing behind her, hopped up and down from foot to foot in excitement.

"Just a minute! Just a minute! You don't know where the photos of Fran are. It'll take hours if you try and find them! Move over. Let *me* have the chair. I'll find the right photos!" cried Elodea, ejecting Priscilla from the seat of power with main force. She accomplished this rather easily since Priscilla had not expected this assault. Priscilla tried to protest but on discovering that the card had one hundred and fifty photos on it, most of them dark and empty smudges, she had to admit that Elodea would find the correct ones more quickly.

So Priscilla leant over her friend's shoulder and looked at the incomprehensible grey outlines on the photos that Elodea selected. They looked like nothing at all to her.

"See! That *has* to be *Fran*," exclaimed Elodea.

Priscilla wondered if Elodea appeared to be convinced of this because her imagination was so good or whether she, Priscilla, should perhaps get her own optician to check the prescription of her spectacles. But then she fortuitously remembered that she had a very good reason not to be able to identify Fran.

"It's impossible for me to say!" she said.

"Why?" asked Elodea.

"If you applied your brain *at all* you would already know that," answered Priscilla in her severest 'ignorant student in tutorial' tone, "for, as you very well know, I have *never seen* Fran!"

"So you haven't!" cried Elodea, cheerful and quite unabashed. "I had entirely forgotten that! But, see, it *has* to be her. She's all muffled up, of course. She must be wearing her old greatcoat again, clearly. Goodness knows, she's probably got all those guns and things back underneath it as well!"

The central grey blur in the shots could, Priscilla supposed, be the figure of *someone*, but if that was the case then it could be anyone on Planet Earth. Elodea seemed quite convinced that it was a human and, assuming this was correct, it was also true that whoever it was had remained sitting in the opposite hedge, outside Elodea's house, for several hours last night, according to the time on the camera shots which had, presumably, been taken every time the human stretched itself or adjusted its position. If the human *was* Fran then, in Priscilla's opinion, her motive for sitting there was most unlikely to be good. If it *wasn't* Fran, then who could it be? Was there *any* possible *good* reason for sitting in the hedge outside the Old Vicarage all night? Priscilla found herself unable to produce one. *Quod gratis asseritur, gratis negatur*. Priscilla thought for a while.

Elodea sat in silence, waiting, hopefully, for her friend to come up with a reassuring suggestion on why Fran might be sitting there and why therefore everything might all be safe and above board, and Elodea could go home and not worry.

"I have a plan!" Priscilla finally pronounced.

"Yes?" said Elodea.

"Where is John at present?" asked Priscilla.

"In France," replied Elodea, "I *think*. Or it could be Germany? Somewhere European because he is in nearly the same time zone as us. Maybe Italy? No, I think it's Switzerland when I consider the matter. Wherever it is, he isn't back till Monday."

"*Conference*?" asked Priscilla.

"*Meeting*! Extended meeting with workshops," replied Elodea.

"*Fortunate!*" said Priscilla. "Because in that case I can come back with you to Little Wychwell and we can spend the night in your house watching the road outside to see who passes along it, or sits there or whatever. It's going to be full moon tonight, so we should be able to see very well! Then we can ascertain firstly if it *is* Fran and, secondly, if it is we can see what she is *doing* out there. Other than sitting, that is."

"That is an *excellent* idea!" said Elodea. "And I won't be at all frightened going back to my house if you are *with* me. Fran won't try abducting me if someone else is there. I'm sure she won't! If you hadn't suggested that you come back with me I was going to ask you if I could stay here."

That, thought Priscilla, was a very close shave. Well worth the trauma of going to Little Wychwell to avoid Pippy and Elodea staying here and wrecking my lovely house!

"Do you have a convenient window for watching the lane?" asked Priscilla, remembering the high hedge that divided the lane from the Old Vicarage garden.

"We will have to go up to the attics!" said Elodea. "You can see the road really well from up there! What fun!"

Priscilla was more dubious about the 'fun' element. She knew that Elodea's stairs definitely did not go up to any attics, so that undoubtedly meant tackling a trapdoor and a ladder.

However, Priscilla, now desperate to regain control of her own hijacked computer, said aloud, "Right! Good plan! We don't need to leave just yet. It won't be dark for hours. So if you don't mind I will just finish my little homily on the Pantheon and send it off to the Prevaricator. I don't want him to miss his daily instalment of information, and it shouldn't take more than half an hour. I had better get it finished. *Ut biberet quoniam esse nollet.* Perhaps you would like to go back downstairs while I do it. You can make yourself at home. Have some more coffee or something."

"Yes, and I'll get Pippy in from the car. She'll be so much more comfortable in the lounge!" said Elodea.

Priscilla pulled a face at the back view of her friend at this suggestion, but Elodea was already skipping down the stairs. Priscilla was so itching to return to the absorbing topic of unsupported concrete domes and the marshes of Rome, with which she was dealing today's knockout blow to that foolish economist, that she decided not to attempt a protest.

Two and a half hours later she descended to find Elodea stretched out on the pure white sofa, her feet on the arm and Pippy on her stomach, bending the spine of one of Priscilla's books back far too far as she perused it.

"Such a wonderfully peaceful room," said Elodea. "Pippy and I *have* enjoyed ourselves! I didn't think you'd mind if I used one of your bowls as a water bowl for her."

"Not at all," said Priscilla, as her gaze fell on an expensive porcelain bowl sitting in a puddle of spilt water in the middle of the carpet. Priscilla reflected momentarily on all the reasons why she usually chose to meet her friend in the neutral and safe venue of an Oxford coffee house. She *must* get Elodea and her infernal hound out of her house *at once*!

"I'll just grab my things," said Priscilla, dashing back upstairs and returning five minutes later with a bulging overnight bag. She was not expecting to stay in Little Wychwell for long but from past experience one never knew. "Let's go!" she cried. "Right away!"

"Hang on, Pris!" said Elodea. "There's no rush, like you said. I'll just take Pippy out in your back garden so that she is comfortable and doesn't get sick on the way back. Don't want her sick on your lap!"

Priscilla shut her eyes in pain at this appalling thought, and agreed.

Elodea seemed to take an unnecessary amount of time in getting Pippy onto her lead and out in the garden and back again and then into her arms and then discovering that she didn't know where she had put her car keys. She then stopped and retraced her steps around every room in the house and eventually found them in her pocket. By now Priscilla felt that all her carpets could be used as samples to find specimens for a study of the natural history of Little Wychwell.

At last they reached the moment that Priscilla was now labelling mentally as "Hazardous Substances Removal". Priscilla, and Elodea, carrying Pippy, headed towards the front door at once. They were then forced into a short session of "after you"s and finally piled through Priscilla's front door both at once, got jammed together within the frame, struggled to disentangle themselves, finally escaped onto the pavement, and then both stopped dead in their tracks.

"Hiya, Lode!" said Fran, who was directly in front of them, leaning nonchalantly against Elodea's car.

Chapter 6

As Elodea, Priscilla and Pippy all stood transfixed, Priscilla and Elodea silent, with mouths slightly open, and Pippy wagging her tail at the sight of a new person to love her, Fran continued.

"I was just wondering how to find you. I wasn't *absolutely* sure *which* house you were in. I've got something most important to tell you 'bout Barnabus! He's in *danger*! We must go and find him immediately!" said Fran.

"How did you know I was here in Oxford?" asked Elodea, regaining her power of speech and noting that Fran was wearing a long grey coat of voluminous proportions, as she had when she was a tramp. She could have quantities of objects hidden under that and so one must assume she was probably armed.

"I've put a tracker on your car, see," said Fran, proudly, "so I could follow you on my iPhone! Let me show you! You can get them to track your dog, see? On second thoughts we don't have any time to show you now! We must find Barnabus at once. Tell me, where is he? Danger! Danger!"

"Barnabus?" said Elodea, trying to force her brain to recover from the shock of walking into Fran and function correctly. "Barnabus? Ah, *Bar*nabus! *Yes*! He must be at *work*! Or, *no*. What is the time?"

"Eighteen hundred hours," said Fran, after looking at her iPhone.

"*Not* at work then!" said Elodea. "Well then, he could be anywhere. I'm afraid I am not my children's keeper!"

"You *must* find him! *Phone* him! Find out where he is!" said Fran.

"He might not answer if he realises it's me. When they realise it's their mother ringing my children always pretend to be unavailable in case I spend too long talking to them," sighed Elodea. "I'll have to text. He'll read that because he knows I don't know he's read it, and if he thinks it's important enough he might even reply as well."

"Are you sure you should do this? Should you tell her where Barnabus is?" hissed Priscilla in Elodea's ear. "It could be a *trick*! *Tu ne cede malis, sed contra audentior ito.*"

Elodea ignored her. One would have thought that Elodea's experience the last time Fran insisted she went somewhere with her and then tried to kill her, would have caused her to dash back inside the house, slam the door and ring the police. One might have also thought that Priscilla would take exactly the same course of action under these unpropitious circumstances. But, despite her words of caution to her friend, Priscilla's detective fever had been reactivated by first Barnabus' visit, and then Elodea's, and it was now rising rapidly and in an uncontrollable way. So she did not make any further protests. Elodea's brain was entirely focussed on the words "Barnabus is in danger!" If there *was* any possibility of her son being in peril and if Fran could *possibly* rescue him, then she *must* risk trusting Fran. Elodea got her phone out of her pocket.

"*Don't* tell him about the *danger*!" said Fran.

"Don't you think he should know?" asked Elodea. Even in her current state it struck her that this was *definitely* suspicious.

"We can't tell him! You don't understand! *They* might be tracking his phone, reading his text messages. See, you'll just make things *more* dangerous! They'll move in at once. Hurry up!" Fran said, looking at her watch again.

"But won't it help *them* to know where he is as well?" demanded Elodea. "Surely I shouldn't ask him that either?"

"They already know where he is; they'll be tracking him. It's us that don't know where he is! But you've got to send him a casual sort of text: 'I'm OK. How are you?' and then hope he tells you where he is as a by-the-way part of his answer. Got to use your *brain*, see," said Fran. "Here, we're wasting time. Give *me* the phone. *I'll* do it!"

Fran snatched Elodea's mobile phone before Elodea could stop her.

"I say!" said Priscilla. "Give –"

Elodea kicked her. "Don't annoy her!" she hissed in Priscilla's ear. "She might get a gun out."

At this suggestion Priscilla subsided into silence.

Fran hummed to herself as she typed away on the keyboard and then stood watching the little screen, waiting for Barnabus to reply.

"Here it is!" she said. "Am fine. Just visiting Flipper's grave," she read out, slowly, keeping the phone well out of reach of the other two. "*Where's that?*"

"Wolvercote Cemetery, but I know where that is! I can drive there in a few minutes. I won't need any directions," said Elodea, not at all wishing to ever be 'navigated' by Fran again.

"Better get going then," said Fran, pointing at the car. "*After you*! No, not *you* in the front seat, Mrs whoever-you-are; *I'll* have the front seat! And don't you think of using your phone while you are in the back, calling the police or anything. Remember, I'm *saving* Barnabus. The cops'll just cock it all up and get him killed. I'll hear you if you even get your phone out of your pocket. And don't *you* think of nipping off anywhere else in this car.

You just drive straight to Flipper's grave, Lode! You do *love* your son, don't you? You do *want* to rescue him?"

"Of *course* I do!" said Elodea, nettled at such a suggestion, and thoroughly alarmed at the word "killed" in conjunction with "Barnabus". "I am going *straight* to where he is!"

After a slight delay due to having to untangle Pippy from Priscilla's legs and prevent her from biting Fran, since Pippy also thought that she herself should have the front seat, they all got in. Priscilla was consigned to the back with Pippy bouncing all over her, and Fran sat, important and upright, in the front passenger seat.

Elodea started the car and drove off, heading for Wolvercote Cemetery as fast as the speed limit would allow. Even in an emergency like this she remembered that only vehicles with blue flashing lights or official status are allowed to break the speed limit with impunity. The Banbury Road was, after all, covered with speed cameras.

* * *

As Barnabus walked up the main driveway of Wolvercote Cemetery the sun was shining down upon him. It was quiet there in the late afternoon – only two or three cars parked and a few people tending graves. He looked at the notice directing him to Tolkien's grave and thought, as he always did, that he must go and see it some day. He passed the most recent graves, stopping for a moment to look at the collections of real and artificial flowers, photographs, little statuettes, bright foil windmills, balloons and birthday cards, and had to get out his handkerchief and wipe his nose a couple of times. But Flipper's grave was not in this section of the cemetery. It was further away, in a quieter spot. He supposed his employers had had something to do with the position. For whatever reason, it was situated among much older graves, far less visited and with only occasional bunches of flowers to adorn them. It was peaceful there and quiet. More like the churchyard at Little Wychwell.

He put his cellophane-wrapped flowers, bought hastily from the nearest supermarket, down on the grassy surface.

"Flipper!" he said. "It beats me why any of us come to visit this grave when we know perfectly well you are not in it."

Just for a moment he thought he heard a smothered laugh from a short distance away – *Flipper's* laugh. He looked all around but there appeared to be no one anywhere near him. He must have imagined it.

He was very tired. It was warm there and pleasant and he was alone – no small children, no wife, no bothersome friends and relations.

He looked around again to make sure he was definitely alone.

"Flipper," he said, "if you were *actually* in there I wouldn't desecrate the grave by sitting on it, but I need to think and it looks awfully comfortable right now!"

He sat down on the grave, leant his back on the black granite stone, and shut his eyes. He must think. He needed to think about *the body*. *Was* it Ustin? Was he *mistaken*? Could he possibly have imagined *something else* was a shotgun wound, and if so, *what was it*? Barnabus had been at work all day and just had a long walk from the centre of Oxford. He was exhausted from stress and lying awake considering these matters all night. The summer afternoon was lovely. He could hear birds singing, warbling, singing…

Barnabus was asleep.

He was dreaming that he and Flipper and Paris were on a battlefield. Paris ordered them to advance but there were bullets flying all around. He felt a sharp pain in his chest and he, himself, fell to the ground. Flipper's voice came to him through the noise of the battlefield, calling him, calling him back to life, softly and insistently.

"Buffy! Buffy!"

It was not a shout but a low and penetrating stage whisper. Barnabus opened his eyes, had a momentary shock as he realised he was in a graveyard, and then woke up properly. But the voice from his dream continued.

"Buffy!"

It *was* Flipper's voice. And it was coming from just behind his head, or perhaps below his head. It could not be coming from the grave, *could* it? Had everyone lied to him? Was Flipper really and truly dead and buried there?

"I *am* going mad," he said, out loud to himself. "Even if Flipper *could* speak to me from beyond the veil, he isn't *in* this grave and, furthermore, he is *still alive*!"

"Don't move. Don't look round," said Flipper's voice, *sotto voce*.

"I'm *asleep still*!" Barnabus concluded out loud.

"No you aren't, you moron!" said the voice. "It's *me*! Now just keep very still and shut up! *Hic locus est ubi mors gaudet succurrere vitae*!"

Barnabus felt this whole statement seemed most unlikely from a character in a dream but there was no other rational explanation for this incident. He was obviously still asleep. He must have just got into that funny state where you 'awoke' into another dream. He looked at the scene ahead to see if it looked absolutely real or not.

An old man was walking slowly but purposefully up the main drive. He was leaning heavily on a stick. He kept stopping for breath, straightening up, looking around. He must be visiting his wife's grave, thought Barnabus. Perhaps he came every day, devoted to her still. He felt tears gathering in his own eyes at the pathos of that slow, decrepit but determined walk.

His phone suddenly buzzed in his pocket.

Angel. It must be Angel ringing. There had been a terrible emergency. She was dead. The children were dead. One of the children was dead! He grabbed his phone from his pocket and looked at it. It was Mama. She wanted to know where he was. Why on earth would Mama want to know that? Sometimes she forgot that he was an *adult*! She really didn't need to keep tabs on him all the time!

He typed a quick and rather curt reply. Still, receiving and typing a text had convinced him that this *was* reality. No voices, no dreams; he was just here, leaning on a piece of granite which seemed to be getting quite cold. He started to shift his position.

"No! If you have *quite* finished playing with your phone, keep *still*! Don't move, and keep your head down!" said Flipper's voice.

There was a popping sound, like someone firing a toy 'cork' gun.

The old man clutched his chest, staggered and fell to the floor.

Barnabus, now ignoring the instructions of any imaginary voices about keeping still, and without turning to see behind him, leapt up and dashed towards the fallen man. The poor old boy must be having a heart attack.

But someone else was there, well in front of Barnabus. A stranger had leapt from a nearby parked car. Barnabus saw him bend over the old man, hurry to his car, grab a blanket and what looked like a medical bag, and return before Barnabus could reach him.

Barnabus slowed down to a more acceptable pace for traversing a cemetery. Whoever it was seemed to know what he was doing. Now Barnabus could take the time to glance back to Flipper's grave. It looked as quiet and deserted as when he had arrived. He must have dreamt or hallucinated the whole episode involving Flipper's voice. It was the only possible explanation. He did hope he hadn't starting hearing voices inside his head. Great Aunt Felicity had been given to such things. Perhaps it was a genetic affliction? He continued a few steps and then looked back at the grave again. Should he retrace his steps, check behind the stone? Could someone be hidden there? Perhaps someone had a radio on nearby, in a car or a local garden. Sounds could drift about, sound loud at a distance. Perhaps he had just made the indistinct noises into something like words because he was still drowsing?

That seemed very likely! Seeing the man fall over must have made him wake up fully.

By the time Barnabus reached the place where the old man was lying, tucked up securely in the blanket, his head almost completely concealed beneath the folds, the stranger was just finishing a phone conversation, presumably with the emergency services. He turned and smiled reassuringly.

"It's OK. I'm a doctor. He's had a minor heart attack but he'll be fine. All under control!" the stranger said.

Others were now gathering with Barnabus, assembling in a small, respectful group, keeping a few footsteps away from the sick man. They spoke few words, and those were in very hushed tones to each other, trying not to disturb the invalid.

It seemed a very short time before the ambulance arrived, lights flashing and siren blazing. The crew got out, calm and efficient, lifted the man in, and headed out again. The doctor got into his car, turned it round and followed them.

"Good!" thought Barnabus. The nice doctor must be going to the JR with the poor old man. He had felt a childish thrill of recognition and 'ownership' as he had realised that the ambulance crew were the same ones who had bounced across the meadows to the riverbank when he and Walls had found Ustin, or whoever it was they had found if it wasn't Ustin. He felt that he 'knew' them. It gave him a sense of importance compared to all the other people in the crowd, who did not know them.

As the ambulance pulled out of the cemetery gates he noticed with surprise that he knew two of the people in the crowd.

"Mama!" he said. "And Aunty Pris! What on earth are you doing here?"

Priscilla and Elodea glanced at each other. Then they looked behind them. Fran was nowhere to be seen. She had been with them when they got out of the car, leaving Pippy locked in it, as cemetery rules barred dogs from the place. Fran had been with them when they galloped towards the little crowd, Elodea being convinced that the crowd were surrounding the corpse of her dead son until she saw Barnabus clearly alive, his head and shoulders rising above the shorter mortals. They had both heard Fran say "Oh, that's all OK now then! Danger over!" but neither of them had seen Fran go because Priscilla had been looking at the ambulance and Elodea had been looking at Barnabus. They were both still out of breath from the rush from the car.

The same thought occurred to both of them. Barnabus would be most annoyed if he discovered that his mama had been stupid enough to get in a car with Fran again, after the time when Fran had tried to drown her. Priscilla also thought that he would be even more angry with someone who seemed to have encouraged his mama to get into the car with Fran than he was with his mama for doing so.

"Why?" they said, in untruthful but identical chorus, "we had just popped up here to visit" whereupon Elodea finished the sentence with the words: "Flipper's grave!" and Priscilla with the words: "Dr Templar's grave. *Viva enim mortuorum in memoria vivorum est posita.*"

At first Priscilla felt annoyed with herself for not saying *Flipper's* grave, and then remembered that officially she didn't even know Flipper so it was just as well she had said someone else. Barnabus was looking at them in some confusion himself. His visit to the cemetery had been bizarre in the extreme so far, and now Mama and Priscilla had turned up to visit the grave of some Oxford don called something that he didn't catch. Did he have to go and visit the grave *with* them to be *polite*, he wondered.

"Sorry, I didn't catch the name. You're visiting Dr *who*?" he said.

"Dr Templar," Priscilla swept on, never having learnt to keep lies to a minimum. "He was a most eminent Classics don who died recently at the age of 99. *Plenus annis abiit, plenus honoribus*! I must go and pay my respects."

Elodea was fairly certain that Dr Templar had never existed and thus had no grave, so she decided to repeat her original lie, which had been drowned out by Priscilla's, in case Barnabus otherwise decided to come to the graveside of Dr Templar with them both.

"Whereas," Elodea announced, firmly, "I just gave Priscilla a lift up here because I have been visiting her. She is *walking back* to her house for *exercise*. I haven't come to visit Dr Templar's grave. I thought I would pop and see Flipper's grave with you since you said you were here. So sad! So young! Poor Flipper! Then I thought if you were still here I could give *you* a lift back to your car at the park-and-ride, and maybe you would like to come and eat dinner with me since Angel and the children are away!"

She thought that he must still be very sad about Flipper – sad enough to think that random joggers who looked a bit like Flipper were his friend. He should not be going home alone after visiting the cemetery.

"Dinner! That's a good thought!" said Barnabus, who had already had every intention of calling round to the Old Vicarage speculatively in the hope of being fed. "I'll just come to Flip's grave with you first then. I was visiting it when this poor man had a heart attack. But he's off in the ambulance now. He'll be fine!"

He galumphed off to Flipper's grave ahead of his mama. He must check. He must make absolutely sure that

Flipper in the flesh definitely wasn't there before she arrived. So awkward if he turned out to be still hanging around, waiting to speak to Barnabus about bodies in rivers and that kind of thing.

"Now I'll have to catch the *bus* back!" said Priscilla to Elodea.

"Well at least you don't have to go and find a grave that *happens* to have the name Dr Templar on it first!" retorted Elodea.

"How did you know Dr Templar didn't exist?" asked Priscilla.

"Experience and guesswork!" replied Elodea.

"Barnabus fell for it, anyway!" said Priscilla. "And he clearly didn't see Fran or he would have mentioned it."

"Let us hope so! *Acta deos numquam mortalia fallunt*," said Elodea to Priscilla.

"I don't think Barnabus qualifies for deification!" snapped Priscilla.

They both felt silly. They both knew that Fran had severe mental problems, so why had either of them believed a word she had said? They both felt thankful that she had vanished again, and neither of them had the smallest inclination to start looking for her.

"I suppose she was hanging around outside the Old Vicarage at night waiting to feed me her story about Barnabus being in danger. And then she found me in Oxford instead. I do hope she doesn't reappear again too soon," said Elodea. "The poor thing – she needs care and love! I wonder if her parents can really manage her these days. They must be getting on a bit! Do you think they get any assistance in caring for her?"

"Do not," said Priscilla, "get it into your head that you need to go and ask them if they need any help. Just keep right away from that woman! *Anything* could have happened this afternoon! *Abundans cautela non nocet*!"

Elodea decided not to remind Priscilla that taking an excursion with Fran had been as much Priscilla's fault as her own, and that she had not heard Priscilla utter a suggestion about being cautious until now.

"Que sera sera!" Elodea said. "Hope you get back OK. I'd better get after Barnabus!"

Priscilla glared at her friend's retreating back. She supposed she had to go and stroll round the cemetery now so it *looked* as if she was visiting *some grave or other*, and then she had to puff out to the nearest bus stop and try to find a bus. Vulcanised. Undoubtedly! At least it wasn't raining.

It was not till much, much later, when he was back in his own house, lying in his own bed, that Barnabus suddenly realised what had really happened in the cemetery. Either Flipper or else the supposed doctor had *shot* the supposed old man. Then he thought about the ambulance crew. *The same crew*. The same crew who had collected Ustin's body.

Everything became clear to him.

But he couldn't tell anyone. He couldn't tell any of his doubters why this proved that he was not mad and that the man in the river *had* been Ustin. He couldn't tell Mama, or Aunty Pris, or Angel. Because they all believed that Flipper was dead.

Finn knew that Flipper was alive. But he couldn't discuss it with *him* for obvious reasons. Finn was evidently part of the whole cover-up.

He was forgetting: Walls *also* knew that Flipper was alive. Now, that was another odd thing. *Why* did Walls know that Flipper was alive? He had never got to the bottom of that one. Peculiar. Presumably Finn had told Walls as well as telling Barnabus? Had Finn told the whole crew? The *whole rowing eight*? If so, at least four *other* people knew that Flipper was alive? *Surely not*!

But *Walls* knew that Flipper was alive, so Barnabus *could* tell Walls all about what had happened this afternoon. Then he considered the matter further. He imagined telling Walls that Flipper had been speaking to him from behind his gravestone, and that a person had then had a heart attack and been taken to hospital, but that he, Barnabus, believed that Flipper had shot him from behind the gravestone. He could hear Walls' voice now, calm and soothing: "Buffy, old fellow, you have to take more rest. You are overworking! You need a holiday! I can, er, *lend* you the money for one, if you like. You know I have plenty of money. It would be nothing to me. L*end*, not give, if that makes you feel any better. You can write me an IOU and pay me back *fifty years hence*! You need to take Angel and the children away for a couple of weeks. You need a *break*!"

Then more dreadful thoughts struck Barnabus. *Why* had Flipper killed someone in the cemetery? Who was the old man? *Why* had Flipper been there waiting for himself, Barnabus, to appear? The answer to that seemed horribly obvious, if chilling. The old man was clearly not an old man – that was simple. The 'stick' was presumably concealing a sniper rifle or similar weapon. Ergo the 'old man' was a killer with a target to kill, in which case there were only two people he could have been aiming to assassinate, when Barnabus considered the choice available in the cemetery crowd. Mostly harmless ordinary people, he would not have been aiming at any of them. There were only two extraordinary people there, according to Barnabus' own egotistic reckoning. Either it had to be Flipper, which was understandable, given his job, or else…

Barnabus gulped. Or else the 'old man' was coming to assassinate himself, Barnabus! In which case Flipper had saved him. But why had he himself become a target? And who was trying to kill him? This *proved* that the dead man had been Ustin. Ustin's gang must think that Barnabus had been responsible for Ustin's death. Flipper and friends, knowing this wasn't true, felt honour-bound to protect Barnabus. Yes, that was it! But a hitman? He could be 'hit' at any time. Barnabus felt a cold sweat down his back. So many hitmen, so few targets. Or were there many, many targets and not enough hitmen? One could only hope that Ustin's gang had blown their entire 'hitman' budget on the previous attempt. How much did it cost to hire one? It must be a *lot*; such a risky and unpleasant profession. Thousands? Millions? Maybe he belonged to the gang and they had only had that one hitman? But Barnabus shivered, even though, at the same time, he had an odd feeling of importance, of being someone so big-league that people would pay money to try and kill him.

He pictured himself telling these *next* ideas to Walls. He could visualize Walls' face – kind, patient but fighting to conceal his horror at the evident state of his friend's mind. Walls would wonder whether to ring for the men in white coats straight away. Then Walls would decide that money could always buy happiness and cure everything, so he would offer to buy Barnabus and his family tickets for a world cruise on a luxury liner so Barnabus could take a long enough rest and recover his sanity. Barnabus giggled for a few minutes, alone in the darkness, and then, despite having realised he had nearly been assassinated that afternoon and was probably still on a hit list, fell into a deep and peaceful sleep.

A few hours later he awoke. Angel was lying in bed at his back. He could hear her breathing. Then he remembered that Angel was away in Northumbria. He was wide awake at once, listening carefully.

There was definitely the sound of someone else breathing next to him. Could a cat have got in through the open window? Did cats breathe that loudly? Had Angel come back for some reason? That must be it. Angel must have returned earlier than expected with the children, for some reason or other. Maybe her work had rung and asked her to come back because someone else was ill. He must have been so heavily asleep that he had not awoken when they came into the house, and she had slipped into bed to surprise him when he did wake up.

He turned over. He could see the curved form of her body even though it was very dark in the room. He extended his arm and put it around her, hoping not to wake her. She must be very tired.

"Oh *good*!" said Flipper's voice, in sarcastic, silky dulcet tones. "You *are* awake! But you don't need to be *so* affectionate!"

"*Flipper*!" exclaimed Barnabus, sitting upright and glaring at the other figure. How could he ever have thought that the other person was Angel? The dark shape was far too big to be Angel. Flipper was sitting up, leaning on the headboard of the bed, and Barnabus had only looked at the recumbent portion of his body and thought it was the whole of Angel.

"It's a comfort," said Flipper, "to know that you are such a good Christian that you even extend kindly feelings towards people who invade your bedroom at night – burglars, kidnappers and the like. No, don't put the light on!"

"How long have you been sitting there?" demanded Barnabus.

"Only a minute or two!" answered Flipper. "You looked so peaceful that I thought I would get my breath back before I woke you up."

"Your breath back?" asked Barnabus.

"Climbing that wall was not an easy task. You should get that drainpipe strengthened up. Thought it was going to come down with me for a nasty moment. And have you tried squeezing in through the top half of a sash window? The things I do for *you*, Buffy, old chap!" replied Flipper.

"My house is not designed to make life easy for cat burglars. The drainpipe is not intended for climbing," retorted Barnabus. "*Most* visitors understand the correct use of doorbells, door knockers and telephones, and also the conventional hours during which one should pay social calls."

"Ah, well," said Flipper, unruffled, "*most* people! Most people, however, are not dead, like me. Being a ghost gives me special rights of breaking and entry, you know! We ghosts follow entirely different social conventions. Our normal visits occur between, say midnight and 4.00 a.m. Have you not considered that?"

"Are you just here to engage in light conversation," asked Barnabus, "or do you have some purpose in giving me such a shock? I have to work tomorrow; I would like to remind you of that. I presume you ghosts don't do a lot of work in the spirit world."

"No, nothing important. I just thought I'd pop in for a chat! Not!" Flipper responded. "Now you are properly awake and your brain is functioning on 'awake', I wanted to have a little chat about our mutual friend Fran. Tell me now. Tell me everything you know about her!"

"*Fran?*" asked Barnabus. "I don't know *anything* about Fran! Nothing that you couldn't find out by using one of your usual channels, anyway."

"Oh, I've used them," replied Flipper, "but I want a personal view, from someone on the spot, and I want the truth, Buffy, not some sanitised statement made by you or your mama or Priscilla or Cyril Blomfeld or Fran's long-suffering parents or anyone else, criminal or otherwise, to someone in authority."

"I'll try," said Barnabus, "but it's…" – and here he picked up his phone and stared at it – "*2.00 a.m.* Wouldn't you like to come and haunt me tomorrow evening, say, instead? I haven't seen Fran for years myself. And I didn't know anything about her at the time. If you want to know about Fran, ask Mama!"

"*You'll* do for my purposes! Come on; what do you know? All of it. You can tell a dead man. Dead men can't talk!" said Flipper.

Barnabus leant against the bedhead next door to his dead friend and assembled his thoughts.

"You haven't gone back to sleep, have you?" asked Flipper.

"No, just getting things in the right order!" replied Barnabus. "Are you ready to record this epic?"

"Buffy, Buffy! Whatever makes you think I am recording what you say? That would be infringing upon your civil liberties!" reproved Flipper.

"OK, I'll call it listening then," said Barnabus. "But I no more believe that you aren't either recording or transmitting everything I say than I do that you are on some kind of middle-of-the-night social call! I suppose I can't go and make a cup of coffee first? No?"

Flipper did not respond to that suggestion.

Barnabus sighed, a long heartfelt sigh. "I could tell you a lot better if you let me have a coffee, and maybe a couple of biscuits, first. Do you want a coffee yourself? I tell you what: we could make a big pot of coffee and we could fry some bacon and have it with fried bread, and then chat in the lounge."

But Flipper remained silent and motionless, waiting for Barnabus to start telling him about Fran.

"I can see how you frighten your suspects into spilling all the beans now!" said Barnabus with another deep sigh. "You are a scary person sometimes; did you know that?" Another lugubrious sigh. "Are you sitting comfortably then, Flipper, my friendly ghost? Once upon a time…"

So Barnabus recounted all he knew about Fran, which can be found by the reader in *Did Anyone Die?* and *A Very Quiet Guest*: the story of her dismissal from the army following drunken behaviour after stress in Bosnia; her descent into living as a drug-addicted tramp in and around Oxford and in the woods near Little Wychwell; her being recruited by Ustin as a drugs courier, and her part in the murder of Jason; her obsession with Ustin, leading to her attempted murder of Elodea, whom she believed Ustin loved; and then he ended with his version of her recent and surprising appearance on Elodea's Facebook page and her visit to Little Wychwell.

"What does Fran do for a *living* then?" asked Flipper. "*These* days, not in the past!"

"How the **** should I know that?" asked Barnabus, who was now thirsty, tired and grumpy at the thought of how little sleep he was going to get before he had to go to work. "I've told you everything I know! She's certified insane, isn't she? Presumably she gets some kind of disability allowance? Or maybe her parents keep her? Now can I go to sleep again so I get a couple of hours in a row before I have to go to work. Or if not, can I at least go and get some coffee?"

"Ah, yes, she gets welfare benefits. You are quite right. But she shouldn't; she shouldn't! Not with *her* income. She has at least *two* jobs," said Flipper helpfully. "One of them is to write online reviews– mostly book reviews."

"She writes online reviews? For books?" said Barnabus, astonished. "Why would anyone pay her to do that?"

"Authors pay her, then she writes good reviews of that particular author's books, and bad reviews of their rival author's books, usually under at least five different names. Ten if they pay her enough. Lots of that sort of job about. You could do it yourself. Little income supplement! She also writes similar reviews for online products. Paid cash in hand through agents who, if you could trace the trail, would lead back to the producers of the aforesaid products. Quite a nice little earner she has there," replied Flipper. "But, now, *what is her other job*?"

"You made that reviewing job up!" said Barnabus. "You *must* have! As if I would do that sort of thing myself! Or anyone would! No one would do that! And why on earth would I know what her *other* job is? Almost certainly something unsavoury and most probably vicious, judging by her past life. Unless she has reformed so far that she has now got religion and writes a religious blog. That's it! Following her successful religious blog she also writes religious articles for journals? No, wait! I definitely have it this time! She writes a blog about being a reformed criminal and is now paid to sit on a whole set of criminal advisory panels and boards? Is *that* it? Have I got it *now*? *Please* can I go back to sleep?"

Barnabus paused to see if Flipper would answer but nothing happened so Barnabus continued his speech, sounding increasingly like a fractious toddler whining.

"Look, Flip, it's lovely to see you again but I am starting to get the impression that you have just called in to annoy me! I've told you *everything* I know about Fran. I hardly know the **** woman! You clearly aren't going to tell me *anything* you know about *anything*, so if you don't want to have a coffee yourself, then at least go away and let me go and get myself one or let me go back to sleep! I'm *tired*!"

"OK, OK, *calm it*!" said Flipper, "I *was* joking about Fran getting *paid* for the reviews she writes but she certainly writes them. All over the Internet. According to her case history files her psychiatrist feels this is a useful way for her to channel her feelings of rage and frustration in a harmless way. I doubt whether the authors and producers for whom she writes bad reviews feel the same way about her vitriolic outpourings and their possible effect on their sales. But for some reason online sites tolerate this sort of nonsense, so who am I to judge? For now, let's assume that activity *isn't* an income source. So! *Think back to what she was wearing when she met your mother* – clothes *most* unsuitable for running across the countryside, not just because of their design but because of their exclusivity and price. Jimmy Choo shoes, for starters!"

"*I* didn't say *Jimmy Choo* shoes!" protested Barnabus. "I said 'red high-heeled shoes'."

"Indeed, so you did, Buffy," replied Flipper, "but *I* say they were Jimmy Choo red high heeled shoes! The rest of her outfit was of a similar price range. If it was not for the fact that your very charming and delightful mama is so unworldly I am sure she would have noticed and transmitted these facts to you herself."

"Mama wouldn't notice things like that," agreed Barnabus. "Maybe Fran's parents buy her expensive clothes. They are well enough off to do so."

"Well enough off, *yes*!" agreed Flipper. "Likely to buy those sorts of clothes, *no*! They belong to the olde-worldly careful upper middle class. Good quality solid clothes, bought to last, even though very expensive – the Saville Row tailored variety of clothes. There is no entry anywhere in their financial statements that would suggest they give their daughter enough money to cover anything extravagant. They buy everything she requires and give her very small pocket money sums for her own expenditure. Thus they make sure that she can buy sweeties if she wants to but she cannot buy anything like alcohol or drugs."

"Maybe she shoplifted them?" suggested Barnabus.

"Not as far as I can ascertain," replied Flipper. "She paid for the red Jimmy Choos with cash."

"She's drug dealing again then!" said Barnabus.

Flipper disregarded this last statement. "Fran's been seen again hanging around Little Wychwell. Perhaps she doesn't only come here to visit your mama? Could she be having a clandestine affair with a rich inhabitant? Is there a rich old man who would fancy a bit of rough with a good looking ex-tramp? This is the sort of information for which I wish you to search your peanut sized brain. Village gossip, Buffy – such a useful source of intelligence!"

"There aren't any possible candidates in this area for that!" said Barnabus.

"Are you *sure*?" asked Flipper.

"No one who would pay her that much money, unless one of the apparently *poor* old men has a fortune stuffed in his mattress and she is breaking into his house and extracting some of it each time she comes here. Most of the rich people in this village are widows, and not lesbian widows, to the best of my knowledge!" replied Barnabus. "I haven't heard anything about any affair with anyone, and since the whole village still perceive Fran to be a tramp it would certainly be hot gossip if *anyone* was conducting any sort of relationship with her. They'd never manage to keep it quiet in Little Wychwell. Hedges have ears; stones have ears. Even the air has ears, if you ask me."

"Your mother now, has she got money to give away to the undeserving poor? Or her friend in Oxford, your Aunt Priscilla?" cooed Flipper.

"Mama doesn't have much spare cash of her own. Dad keeps her on a small allowance because she does indeed, as you say, have a tendency to give it away to all manner of charitable causes, deserving and otherwise. Fran might be able to bamboozle some money out of her but Mama doesn't have enough spare to fund that sort of footwear. Priscilla's probably sitting on a nice little nest egg of her own earnings and she certainly buys expensive clothes for herself, but she doesn't let the moths out of her purse for other people. I can't imagine she gives Charles any of her money. I would imagine that if any money passes between them, she takes it off him. Priscilla can probably afford the odd pair of Jimmy Choos, even if they aren't quite her style, but she would only buy them if they were going to be put on her own feet! And she most definitely wouldn't give anything to Fran. If she gives anything to *any* charity I am guessing it would be a charity to preserve the teaching of the Classics," replied Barnabus.

Flipper glanced at his watch. "The time is *racing* past," he said. "How it flits away when you have a chat with an old friend! But I don't want to overstay my welcome. Been *lovely* talking to you, Buffy, old chap. Just consider me to be a dream that passed in the night. I'm not real, you know! But could you possibly close the very real window behind me? Cheerio!" And he opened the sash window to its fullest extent, slid out silently and vanished without a sound.

By the time Barnabus had got out of bed and crossed the room to close the window Flipper had dissolved completely into the moonless darkness, like the phantasmal vision that he claimed to be.

Barnabus looked at the clock – 2.30 a.m. He thought it was later than that. He was thirsty and grumpy. What was Flipper up to? What was Fran up to? Whatever it was, he knew he couldn't talk to anyone else about any of this conversation. Flipper took liberties! He might be dead but he had no excuse for this sort of behaviour, waking people up in the middle of the night for no particular reason. Barnabus didn't think anyone could possibly be having an affair with anyone as old and insane as Fran. Could Flipper have been putting ridiculous ideas into the conversation to distract Barnabus from realising what it was that Flipper had actually wanted to know? Barnabus ran back over what he had said in his own mind. Nothing of importance that was not recorded elsewhere in the police records, or the mental health files. He didn't suppose Flipper and his ilk were concerned about the confidentiality of data in any files that they wanted to read. He must get Mama to describe those red shoes more exactly tomorrow. Then he could look them up and see if they were indeed likely to be Jimmy Choos, and if so, how much such things would cost.

It was only then that he realised he had now seen Flipper twice in one day and missed *two* opportunities to ask him to confirm that the body in the river was Ustin and explain what exactly the body was doing in the river and who had shot him. Had *Flipper's* side shot him, or the *other* side, whoever the mysterious others might be? Even worse, he had now missed *one* opportunity to ask who the man in the cemetery was and why anyone had been trying to shoot him, himself, Barnabus, and how to best avoid getting shot in the future.

Barnabus felt very tired but was equally certain that he would never sleep again that night. If he got up now and had a big breakfast and then drove straight into Oxford he could join Walls on his early morning run. Walls never minded what time his friends turned up to visit, and Yvette could just do the other thing if she objected to his appearance around 5.00 a.m. Yes, go and get some exercise. Forget Flipper; forget all the nonsense! Perhaps he and Walls could even have a pre-breakfast row in a Kings College coxless pair? Walls would be rude about the fact that Barnabus was out of practice but that didn't matter. Barnabus felt that hard exercise was what he needed it to put his head straight.

* * *

Flipper was leaning against a gate, just around the corner, talking to No-one.

"Origin of designer items confirmed unlikely to be Elodea, Priscilla or anyone from Little Wychwell and surrounding villages," he said.

"Confirmed then. Continue as instructed. Remember suspect's training and probability of being armed," said No-one in Flipper's ear.

Chapter 7

On the previous evening Elodea had no sooner dropped Barnabus at the park-and-ride to retrieve his own car than she pulled into a spare parking space, out of her son's sight, and rang Priscilla.

"*Ave*!" said Priscilla, who had only just managed to get onto a bus and was now riding down the Banbury Road. She had groaned aloud at the sight of the number on her mobile, much to the surprise of the person next to her, but decided she had better answer it. Maybe something actually *had* happened? At the word *Ave* her neighbour on the bus seat realised that Priscilla was foreign. That explained the groan. You never knew what foreigners might do next.

"*Ave*!" replied Elodea. "We are still on for tonight, aren't we?"

"For tonight? Why? What are we doing tonight?" asked Priscilla.

"Watching the lane! In case Fran is there!" said Elodea. "You must remember that! We only arranged it this afternoon!"

"I know we did. But presumably she was sitting outside your house waiting to talk to you. She saw you today.

She spoke to you. Everything she said was complete and utter nonsense, but she has talked to you. QED," replied Priscilla.

"We don't *know* that!" protested Elodea, who had been reconsidering the position. "Just because she spoke to us today doesn't mean she won't be out there *again* tonight! I agree that what she told us this afternoon was clearly gibberish; there was nothing whatsoever wrong with Barnabus and she must have known that. That was why she vanished so quickly when we saw him. But isn't that sort of behaviour an indication that her mental state is quite unstable? She might do *anything*!"

"Get Barnabus to sit up with you then!" huffed Priscilla.

"I can't! I can't possibly tell him that you and I let Fran get in my car with us, especially now that we know that what she said to us was utter nonsense!" moaned Elodea.

"Point taken!" said Priscilla.

"And we have no idea what she might take it into her head to do next! If she realises I am in the house on my own she might come in while I am in bed just so she can talk to me again!" wailed Elodea.

"Lock the doors then!" said Priscilla, heartlessly.

"No, Pris, you *know* you *agreed* to come round. Come on! It'll be *fun*! Like the old days at college! We can eat biscuits and drink gin!" begged Elodea.

"I suppose I have to!" replied Priscilla. "But haven't you got Barnabus in the house already?"

"Yes, yes. He's coming round for dinner but he'll go home later. I'll ring you when I've throw him out, and you can drive round then," said Elodea. "By the way, is there something wrong with your phone?"

"No!" said Priscilla. "Nothing wrong with it!"

"There just seems to be a funny buzz in the background," said Elodea.

"That," said Priscilla, with great dignity and majesty, "is because I am on a bus. If you recall, you volunteered me to catch a bus back home! As in *Caesar sic in omnibus*, you know!"

Elodea giggled politely at Priscilla's Latin joke and continued, "I'm so sorry, Priscilla. You know it was an emergency. We couldn't tell Barnabus about Fran! I would have given you a lift back as well if it wasn't for you being supposed to be visiting Dr Templar's grave. I *assume* you *found* it?"

"Elodea Smith, many people who do not know you well think you are a *kind and lovely* person who would not lower herself to use *sarcasm*!" said Priscilla.

There was a sound of smothered giggles from the other end.

"Very well then," continued Priscilla, who could not prevent herself from feeling quite excited at the thought of this late-night 'spooking', "I will await your phone call with eagerness. But get rid of that son of yours a.s.a.p. Otherwise, if you don't get a reply to your call you can assume I am already in bed and asleep, and you can watch for Fran all by yourself!"

"OK, OK!" said Elodea. "I tell you what: just arrive at 10.00 p.m. I'll make sure Barnabus has gone by then and save dinner for you as well, and you can eat when you get to the Old Vicarage."

"Very well. *Vale!*" said Priscilla, and she pressed the 'end of call' button.

She had been vulcanised again, without a shadow of a doubt. Vulcanised! She really must develop some better resistance to vulcanisation for the future. But having a midnight party in the attic in Elodea's house did sound like a return to their youthful days. She quite fancied being silly and young again herself. Also Elodea's cooking was extremely good.

Barnabus was quite surprised to be summarily dismissed and sent home at 9.30 p.m. His mama told him that she was taking an early night.

"Are you feeling well, Mama?" he asked.

"Yes, quite well!" she replied. "But I was up very early today and I am tired. Also you look exhausted yourself.

Have a lovely night's sleep without those children hopping in and out of bed all night. Here, take another portion of apple crumble with you, and let me cut you a chunk of cake to take as well."

"Thank you, Mama!" said Barnabus and, taking his goodies, he trotted off to his own house.

Ten minutes later Priscilla's car drew up outside the Old Vicarage, and rolled in neutral silence for the last few yards to end next door to Elodea's, well inside the stable yard. Priscilla crept out of it and ran, bent double to the back door, where she knocked very quietly three times.

"It's open!" called Elodea loudly from the kitchen.

"Shush!" said Priscilla, reprovingly, as she entered. "I have been trying to effect an unobtrusive entrance in case Fran should already be in the lane!"

"What a good idea!" said Elodea.

Elodea surveyed her friend's dress. Priscilla was wearing a just-above-the-knee A-line skirt, sheer stockings, expensive looking high heels, a perfectly ironed blouse with a lace front, and a smart jacket, the jacket and skirt both being in plain salmon pink and the blouse in snowy white. Elodea was wearing jeans, an old T-shirt and a very old and baggy jumper.

"You do realise that the attics are probably in a bit of a dusty mess?" she said anxiously.

"Yes, indeed. This is why I am wearing *my gardening clothes*!" Priscilla replied, in a surprised tone, only just avoiding adding that Elodea's entire house was, as usual, in a "bit of a dusty mess" and that she had dressed accordingly.

Elodea reflected that Priscilla's gardening activities consisted of snipping off the odd dead head from plants in her tubs. But she changed her mind about offering Priscilla any other clothes to wear.

"I'll take Pippy out for her final walk while you sort out dinner for yourself. Be back in half an hour," said Elodea. "Do you think I should *conceal* your car? I have a whole set of brambles that I clipped off in the garden the other day. Plenty to go over a car your size! No one will notice it is there then!"

The thought of brambles scratching the paintwork was beyond what Priscilla was prepared to endure, even to be a detective again.

"No," said Priscilla, decisively. "No, I don't think the car is very visible from the road, because I put it well back from the road, next to yours. Have a good walk. I'll manage!"

Priscilla had guessed correctly that Elodea had hoped that Priscilla might offer to go with her on the walk and then eat afterwards. But Priscilla would rather tackle foraging for herself in Elodea's kitchen than roaming the muddy paths of a dark Little Wychwell.

Elodea vanished accordingly with Pippy, and Priscilla dined well on goulash and apple crumble. Priscilla was feeling happy and replete by the time Elodea and Pippy reappeared. After several liqueur coffees to give them 'Dutch courage' she and Elodea began their ascent to the attic, bearing with them some biscuits, a bottle of Gordon's gin, a full kettle of water, two cups, coffee, cream and sugar.

They reached the topmost landing. There was the trapdoor, looking far higher above them in the ceiling than Priscilla had hoped.

"Where do you think John keeps the loft ladder?" asked Elodea, doubtfully.

"How should I know?" asked Priscilla, who was out of breath after two flights of stairs. "It's *your* house!"

"Yes, but I don't usually go into the attic. John does that!" said Elodea. "There is always a ladder that's fitted to get up there when he goes up!"

They both looked around the landing but there was clearly no sign of it.

"Maybe the ladder is in the attic?" said Elodea.

"Well, that would be a really stupid place to keep it!" expostulated Priscilla. "How could you get up there to get it down?"

"Yes, but I think that *is* where it is!" said Elodea. "I remember now! John stands on the landing chair and pushes the trapdoor across and then pulls the ladder down!"

"Only a man could possibly think of such a stupid idea," said Priscilla. "He's twenty feet taller than us! How on earth are *we* supposed to get it down? *Tanta stultitia mortalium est*!"

"I suppose John *is* a lot taller than us," Elodea sighed. "I know; I'll go down and get the stepladder! Wait here a minute!"

Priscilla waited as the minutes ticked on and on. Only the Smith family could possibly have misplaced a large object like a stepladder, she reflected, but given the size and entirely untidy nature of their dwelling this could be quite a long wait.

After fifteen minutes Elodea's voice floated triumphantly up the stairs. "I've found it! I'll just get it out from under everything and I'll be with you in a jiffy!"

A series of distant crashes and bangs followed. Priscilla heard Elodea's voice floating up the stairs. It was saying, brightly but firmly, "*No*, put the light fitting down *at once*! *Baaaad stepladder*!"

The poor woman has had *at least* three children too many, Priscilla said to herself, let alone all those grandchildren.

There was series of clunks as the ladder ascended the first flight of stairs, and a collection of crashes as it negotiated the landing, including a sound suspiciously like breaking china. Elodea finally emerged, dusty but still undefeated, at the base of the second flight, and began to wrestle it upwards.

"My head is bloody but unbowed, Pris!" she called. "Soon be there now!"

Priscilla watched the final pitched battle between woman and stepladder and was positively alarmed. Most people would have rushed down to help. This concept did not cross Priscilla's mind. But even she felt moved to say something.

"Elodea! Do be *careful*!" she cried.

"I'm fine!" Elodea replied, firmly. Being fully aware of Priscilla's limitations in any non-academic field and fearing Priscilla might join in and increase the chaos, she added, "Don't come and help; I am having quite enough trouble on my own. *Aut viam inveciam aut faciam*!"

Priscilla did not mind at all about being relegated to just watching the epic struggle, as she had never had any intention of joining in. After heaving the stepladder this far even the normally indefatigable Elodea was tiring but the stepladder was still fresh, bouncy and resolute. Elodea was proceeding backwards up the treads and dragging the stepladder behind her. Every now and then the weight became too much and the stepladder triumphantly descended a few steps again and they had to be repeated. Elodea was not being helped by the ever-loyal Pippy, who had deduced that the ladder was attacking Elodea. Consequently Pippy kept clambering onto whichever step was just above Elodea, and barking and growling at Elodea's opponent. Apart from the noise, Pippy was further impeding matters because Elodea had to keep glancing behind her to see where Pippy was before backing onto the next step.

At last Elodea stood victorious on the landing, with the vanquished stepladder leaning, resigned, against the wall. Once Elodea had ensured it was safely propped there she subsided onto the carpet beside it for a few minutes, breathing hard. Priscilla stood staring at both of them. She wondered for a moment if there was anything she *should* be doing to be helpful but being quite unable to think of what it might be. So she contented herself by saying "*Per angusta ad augusta*!" in a congratulatory tone and returned to thinking about her current 'academic work in progress' and humming to herself. After a while Elodea revived and after a further five minutes managed to get the ladder into its open inverted V position and lock the top step into place.

"So difficult to get that platform to click down properly!" Elodea grumbled, still gasping a little. "But thank goodness it's all done and ready now!"

"What?" said Priscilla, jumping slightly and looking around vaguely. Elodea glared at her but Priscilla did not notice.

Elodea trotted up the stepladder, lifted her arms above her head and, with a few groans as she made the effort to unjam its layer of securing dust and then raise it, finally heaved the   trapdoor upwards. A shower of dead flies and other insect life, muddled up with thick grey sticky wisps of old cobweb, descended onto Priscilla, who had been bounced out of her reverie by the unexpected creaks and groans, and then made the error of looking upwards as the trapdoor opened. As Priscilla spat out a fly, which had dropped directly into her open mouth, she was screaming the word "Vulcanised. Vulcanised!" silently to herself, although she also had to admit the fact that this vulcanisation had been entirely voluntary on her part, nay, even *suggested* by herself. Priscilla began to review her own nearest relatives in an effort to decide if the behaviour of any of them suggested a genetic disposition to insanity. "*Nullum magnum ingenium sine mixtura dementiae fuit*," she comforted herself.

Elodea sprang off the top of the stepladder and, after a few anxious moments when it seemed that gravity was going to prevail, disappeared upwards into the attic, head first. Her feet finally scrabbled through the gap, and she was gone. A few seconds later she reappeared leaning out of the opening, her hair covered with grime and cobwebs, and a dead spider dangling enticingly over one ear.

"I've found the proper ladder now!" shrieked Elodea, excitedly. "It *is* up here! I just have to use this sort of mechanism thing and it will come down to the landing beautifully. I remember it all now. *And* I found the light switch! But you must have noticed that when the light came on. Can you just close the stepladder up, lean it against the far wall and make sure Pippy is out of the way?"

"*Why?*" asked Priscilla, who was carefully looking downwards in case of further accidents with descending debris. "Why don't we *just use the stepladder?*"

"No, no!" said Elodea. "John is always very firm about using the correct ladder! Health and Safety, you know."

"In that case *why does he hide it in the attic?*" demanded Priscilla.

"It will be much easier for you to climb up and down on the *proper* ladder," cajoled Elodea.

"All right, all right," grumbled Priscilla, who had been just about to suggest that she had her own midnight feast and vigil on the landing and talked to Elodea through the trapdoor, "if I *must!*"

She had no idea how she was meant to avoid Pippy while manipulating a ladder about on a very small landing, but Pippy solved this problem for her. Priscilla did not attempt to lift or close the ladder but instead started to push it across the floor. The feet produced such a loud screeching sound that Pippy vanished down to the stairs with a yelp.

The real loft ladder was definitely superior in design and did not require a final leap through the air, or, as would have happened in Priscilla's case, being hauled in an undignified and dangerous manner through the trapdoor by Elodea. However, to Priscilla's satisfaction it was still of a form of step that was still completely inaccessible to very small dogs. Priscilla herself felt rather wobbly as she ascended the narrow treads, but she attempted to be resolute and cheerful, saying "*non est ad astra mollis e terris via*" as she squeezed through the trapdoor, which had clearly been made for people who did not enjoy eating.

Pippy, miffed and upset by being deserted on the landing, curled up miserably around the ladder's base like a small and angry dragon guarding its hoard.

"Bother!" said Elodea, peering downwards. "We will have to remember she is there when we go back down, otherwise we might step on her. Do you think I should carry her up?"

"*No!*" said Priscilla. "Because," she added hastily, and impressed with her own unanswerable idea about why not, "if you do she might accidentally fall down through the trapdoor in the dark and hurt herself! *Caveat!*"

"I suppose she might," said Elodea. "What a shame we can't close the trapdoor without removing the ladder. And it might drop down to the landing instead of rising if we try that – it's done that before now. Do you think that if that happened one of us could jump down there and lift it back up?"

"No," said Priscilla, who was definitely not going to risk her method of escape being removed.

"I suppose it is a *long* drop," said Elodea, looking dubiously down the ladder, "and if one of us got a broken ankle it would be *unfortunate.*"

"*Most!*" agreed Priscilla.

"It's OK, Pippykins!" Elodea called down the ladder. "Mama's only going to be up here for a little while. Oo waits down there, Diddums, till Mama gets back downs! Mama give oo special treaties tomorrow to makes ups!"

Priscilla hoped that her expression did not look too much like her real feelings during this speech, or that if it did, Elodea had not seen it.

"Right!" said Elodea. "She should be fine now! She'll be asleep for the night shortly anyway. We had better be careful that neither of us *falls* down through the trapdoor though, or we might squash poor Pippykins!"

Elodea surveyed the attic, cobweb- and dust-strewn, with mysterious dark bundles and boxes that had clearly been in residence for some years. "What shall we sit on? We'll never carry a chair up that ladder! I could pop down and get some cushions, perhaps?"

"I think we will be fine without," answered Priscilla. "There must be something to sit on in all this pile of jun–, er, *things*, up here! ... Here, this looks good! Give me a hand with this!"

The attic contained many weird, wonderful and almost completely useless things that had been consigned there along with dust, cobwebs and dead spiders, but Priscilla had spotted a familiar looking piece of striped canvas attached to a piece of wood. It was under a pile of boxes but the two of them pulling together managed to get it out and were pleased to discover that it was, indeed, an ancient, tatty but still serviceable deckchair. They found another old deckchair leaning on the wall just behind a long-broken vacuum cleaner that had been kept in case it ever got mended by a psychic phenomenon in the attic. The chairs were just right for people who were trying to see through the very low attic window.

"See! It's a good clear view of the lane from up here, and no one will ever see us up here at this window," said Elodea.

"Definitely not through this layer of detritus!" replied Priscilla, coughing as she leant towards the glass and inhaled an involuntary mouthful of dust. She rubbed a small clean hole on the glass with an old rag she had found on the floor.

"I've just thought! I'll never get that ladder *back up and stowed away again*!" said Elodea. "What is John going to say?"

"Why should he say anything?" asked Priscilla.

"He'll notice I've been in the attic! What can I tell him? I can't mention the word 'Fran' to him! He would go completely dotty if he heard about what had happened this afternoon!"

"Tell him you had lost something and were looking for it in the attic!" said Priscilla.

"*What* something?" asked Elodea.

"I can't solve all your problems! You can think of that!" said Priscilla.

"*I* know!" said Elodea. "I'll take the deckchairs out to the garden. Then I can say I was looking for them so I could sit on them in the garden!"

Priscilla hoped the house would survive this event. Elodea had probably dented anything that could be dented with the stepladder already, so surely she couldn't do much more damage getting two deckchairs downstairs?

"You know, Pris," said Elodea, "I had one of those 'taking my A levels' nightmares again last night. The one where you haven't revised for them and you know you are going to fail. It's funny because A Levels were the easiest exams I ever took. And, I was thinking, if I had nightmares about people calling when I hadn't done the housework, say, that would be much more understandable. So why the A levels?"

Priscilla, who had now had a good look at Elodea's face, was feeling nervously round her own ears to see if she also had a spider for an earring. "What?" she said.

"I was just saying that I had a nightmare about... Oh, never mind! You know what, this reminds me of that night in the first year when we couldn't get to sleep after we had been to that disco," replied Elodea.

"Disco?" said Priscilla. "I don't believe I ever went to such a thing in my life!"

"Yes, you did!" said Elodea. "Don't you remember? It was at…"

Thus they passed a pleasant enough couple of hours, reminiscing, or rather with Elodea reminiscing and Priscilla making hopefully suitable noises every now and then. Both of them were sharing the gin bottle and the biscuits and the coffee. Every now and then they remembered why they were there, and glanced into the lane every now and then, but discovered no evidence of any human or mammalian life there, excluding bats. Moths and a few bats and the odd owl swooped past in the air, but no earthbound forms of life appeared. They heard the church clock strike midnight, then the quarter, the half-hour, the quarter, and then, finally, one o'clock.

And then Priscilla and Elodea both became tired of propping themselves on the edge of their deckchairs so that they could crane through the window, and they both leant back in them to "more easily. We can sit up and look out of the window every now and then". After a few more minutes, interspersed with the occasional sentence, their eyelids drooped, their eyes closed, their breathing grew soft and gentle, and they both remained fast asleep till the sun shone brightly on their morning faces.

"ARRGGGHHH," was the cry which awoke Priscilla from a deep and happy dream.

"What?" Priscilla yelled, attempting to sit upright abruptly and nearly folding herself up in her own deckchair. She looked around, completely baffled. "Where am I?"

"In our attic, *remember*!" explained Elodea, who had already sprung out of her chair. "We must have both nodded off! We've missed the whole night! *Am I stiff*!"

Priscilla attempted a more gentle approach to rising from her chair, and failed miserably.

Elodea took pity on her and helpfully heaved her out of it.

"I am not feeling so very flexible myself," said Priscilla. "Well, we've missed anything that happened in the lane by now! *Rides, si sapis*! I am going to attempt to negotiate this ladder and then avail myself of your bath in an effort to freshen up!"

"Yes! Do! There might even be some hot water by now, the boiler takes a while to wake up in the morning's itself these days" said Elodea. "But I'd better go down the ladder first: Pippy, you remember! Be careful stepping on the landing. She may have had an *overnight accident*. I'll take her out into the garden and make breakfast, and by then you'll be ready to eat it! And while I am out there I'll grab the wildlife camera! I expect Fran wasn't there at all!"

Priscilla's face was already a picture of misery at the thought of a cold bath and the possibility of standing in dog excrement. This final statement was the last straw.

"You *set the camera*?" yelled Priscilla. "Why was I sitting in the attic with you then?"

"So we could see *exactly* what happened!" said Elodea. "Remember? And we had such fun reminiscing too!"

"No!" said Priscilla, mumpish, cold, and suffering pins and needles in many places. "I don't remember. As usual, I have no idea why I was persuaded to take part in *any* of your family's totally mad schemes!"

"You'll feel better after breakfast!" soothed Elodea. "*Possunt quia posse videntur!* But do be careful coming down the ladder! You need to get your circulation moving before you try it!"

As Elodea bounced springily and joyfully down the ladder, wide awake, happy in the new day she called back, "Wiggle your toes first!"

"Wiggle my toes! I should have wiggled my brain yesterday!" retorted Priscilla, "Whoever first said '*Tu ne cede malis sed contra audentior ito*' was a complete idiot!"

After breakfast, just when they were both meditatively staring at their third cups of black coffee, Elodea had a terrible recollection.

"Priscilla!" she said. "My car!"

"Your car?" asked Priscilla.

"Fran said she had bugged my car!" gasped Elodea.

"Fran said a lot of things, none of which appear to have been at all true," retorted Priscilla.

"I know she did, but she did find me at your house! Perhaps she really *has* put a tracking device on my car!" said Elodea.

"What if she has?" asked Priscilla. "It's not as if you go anywhere at all interesting in it."

"But I don't want her following me about, stalking me!" said Elodea.

"Oh, I see," said Priscilla, vaguely. She didn't think that Fran needed to stalk Elodea since she could usually find her in Little Wychwell Old Vicarage if she wanted to do so. "Can't John find it and take it off? He must have something in his laboratory."

"For goodness sake, Priscilla!" Elodea expostulated. "Just because he works in a laboratory doesn't mean he has things to detect bugs attached to cars! In any case, that would mean telling him about Fran!"

"Barnabus then," suggested Priscilla, hopefully. "One of his friends probably has an app on their phone for that sort of thing."

"We aren't telling *him* about Fran either," Elodea reminded her.

"*I* know!" exclaimed Priscilla. "Angel! She studied Engineering! She must know about these things!"

"Pris," protested Elodea, "if we aren't telling Barnabus we can hardly tell Angel! Anyway, she would go right off the end about Amadeus and Theodora being in danger if we told *her*!"

"Ah," said Priscilla, who had imbibed rather more of the gin than Elodea while in the attic and was feeling the results. Her head now had a relentless and unpleasant drummer resident in it. This seemed much more important than the possibility of a tracking device on Elodea's car.

"Well, don't use the car!" Priscilla concluded.

"Don't use it?" asked Elodea.

"I can't see any other solution," said Priscilla, definitely and with an air of finality.

"I suppose I don't *have* to go out anywhere that's too far to walk," sighed Elodea, "and I can get the supermarket shopping delivered. I *know*! I'll look online and see if there is a 'detect a bugging device' app that I can download for myself, or any other advice on how to find one on your car. Bound to be something somewhere on the Internet. Until then I suppose you are right – I'll just have to not use the car. I'll go and get the camera, and we can both look at the photos."

"*You* can look at the photos," said Priscilla. "I'm off back to Oxford!"

It had just occurred to Priscilla that if her own car stayed in Elodea's garden any longer she might find it had a tracking device planted on it as well.

"No you don't!" said Elodea. "It's only 7.30 a.m. You can't possibly be needed in Oxford before nine thirty or ten. You can come and look at the photos the camera took before you go!"

The photos were the same as the night before – no animals, but just a human figure, which Elodea was convinced was Fran, sitting there in the hedge, until 4.30 a.m., when suddenly there were three figures, all walking off to the right of the picture. Two of the figures were taller and the other figure was sandwiched between them.

"*Who are they?*" they both exclaimed.

"What happens next? What happens next?" asked Priscilla, trying to get control of the mouse.

But there were no more photos with people in them at all, only the usual dawn photos of the local birds.

"Why is that the *only* photo of all three people?" asked Priscilla, excited. "The other two must have got there somehow? Are you sure you didn't miss some earlier ones? And then they must have left as well. Why aren't there more photos? Did the camera malfunction? What a time to choose to do that!"

"Because it's got a time delay between photos, to stop it taking hundreds and hundreds and hundreds of photos if there *was* anything moving about. If you look at the photo before that, you can see that Fran has moved and turned slightly to look behind her. She must have heard them approaching, and that triggered that shot. The other people might have only just been off the frame in that shot. So then there will be a gap before the next photo of the three of them. And a gap after that in which they all had time to get out of the viewfinder," explained Elodea.

"How ridiculous! No wonder you never get any animal pictures! And most unfortunate in this case!" grumbled Priscilla. "Why on earth did you set the interval so far apart? How on earth are we meant to work out who those two other people might be, with only one photograph?"

"It's got an interval because the photos would overflow the card otherwise. At least I thought they would. I remember now: I thought there were so many animals in the garden that I had better set the interval at the maximum so as not to overflow the card. I'd forgotten I'd done that! It doesn't notice usually because there aren't any photos. Didn't you notice that Fran arrives in the hedge without walking past to get there, and then vanishes in the same way? That's because of the interval too," said Elodea, instructively. "But we *are* being silly!" she continued, extrapolating from her own experience with her own children, and the illogical and irrational reason that the two mystery people were both bigger than

Fran, which reminded Elodea of two parents guiding an unwilling child. "I *know* who they must be! It's her *parents*! They must have found out she was out, and then rung her up to find out where, and then come out to get her!"

"Ah!" said Priscilla, thinking that Fran had an unusually enormous mother and that this seemed most unlikely, but it was making Elodea feel happy and would do as well as any other explanation. Furthermore, it would release herself to go back to Oxford. "Brilliant deduction! Well done! That's it: mystery solved. I'm off!"

"You *do* think they were her parents, don't you? That Fran is safe at home now?" asked Elodea, suddenly anxious. Had Priscilla been a little too eager to agree?

Priscilla did not care about the identity of these people in the least. They could be fair or foul, and she did not care what had happened to Fran either except for the academic interest of the detective investigation. Her body was suffering from its uncomfortable night and the fact that she had just been forced to make her ablutions in a bathroom that had not been updated since around 1910. Priscilla saw a golden opportunity to get out of this mad village and the awful plumbing in the Old Vicarage, and go home to her spotless home where the bathroom equipment never malfunctioned.

"Yes, yes, obviously," Priscilla burbled. "Excellent! They will be getting her the care she needs now! They've realised what she is up to! I expect they rang for her psychiatrist the second they got in. Marvellous! Cheerio then!"

Priscilla rushed towards the door and was gone before Elodea could stop her.

Elodea had not drunk as much gin as Priscilla but her head was still aching and she felt queasy too. She stayed in her seat, Pippy curled on her knee, feeling deflated and sad, staring at the photo. The people did look kindly. They were leaning towards Fran. They must be her parents. Poor Fran, she thought, still having to be corralled, limited and rescued by her parents at her age, never being allowed to be a grown-up, and her poor parents too, at their ages, still having to keep an eye on her as if she was a small child. I can't go round and offer to help because I don't have a car till we get this tracker problem sorted out.

It was clear that Priscilla would not be willing to watch from the attic again. John would be back tonight and anyway Fran's parents would surely keep a close watch on her for now. All the same, Elodea thought, she would set the camera again and see what it showed tomorrow.

* * *

The next day in Little Wychwell was uneventful apart from John's return. Elodea managed to get the camera set up in the hedge before bed, and on the following morning she could hardly wait to wave John off to Oxford so that she could check it. John seemed to take an interminable time sorting out things before he left, moving things from his suitcase to his briefcase, forgetting something, coming back in, going again. Finally the car headed out down the lane.

Elodea nipped out to the hedge, snatched the camera and dashed in. She told herself that she was expecting to see no one on these photos at all, unless it was the Vicar. Fran must be being kept safely at home by her parents. But Elodea had a nagging worry in case those two figures were not Fran's parents and that their intent towards Fran was not kindly.

But there Fran was, a little later than usual, for she did not arrive till 3.00 a.m., sitting in the hedge just as before.

"Thank goodness!" gasped Elodea. "Those people *were* Fran's parents last night! But she must have escaped their vigilance and got out again. Perhaps they had both fallen asleep and dropped their guard. I wonder if they are going to turn up in another photo and collect her again. So trying to have to attempt to keep Fran under control, especially at their ages. They must both be getting on a bit."

Elodea carried on scanning through the next few photos, all still Fran. She seemed peaceful enough, sitting in her hedgerow perch. Then Elodea reached a photo taken at 3.30 a.m. There were now two people in the photograph, walking along and carrying something between them. Something that could be a very large bag. But Elodea had seen enough detective series on the television to fear that it might be something much more sinister. Some people had kidnapped Fran and were carrying her off between them. The two standing figures were both too big to be Fran, and Elodea was sure, for some reason, that they were men. Although, when she thought about it, both of Fran's parents had looked very large on the previous night's photo, so it could be them again. Perhaps Fran was already in their car, Elodea reassured herself, and her parents had come back to get a bag Fran had brought with her. Perhaps it contained some things Fran had with her to use during the night: blankets and coffee and whatnot. Why on earth hadn't she got the manual out and worked out how to shorten the delay between photos?

Elodea couldn't use her car to go and check whether Fran was back safely at home because if the mystery figures were not Fran's parents, then whoever they were would not only have kidnapped Fran but would also have Fran's phone. If Fran was telling the truth when she said she could track Elodea's car using this phone, then the mystery people could also track Elodea's car with Fran's phone themselves. Should she ring the police to ask them to check on whether Fran was OK? No, for her story would sound ridiculous in the extreme. Perhaps she should ring Barnabus? No; he would be on the way to work. There was only one possible person that she could ring.

Accordingly Elodea rang Priscilla and as soon as Priscilla answered Elodea asked her to come over to Little Wychwell, *right away*. That was all Elodea had time to say before the doorbell rang.

"Must go and answer the door. I expect it's Wayne, you know, the postman," said Elodea's breathless and worried voice in Priscilla's ear. "Be back with you in a trice!"

Priscilla looked at the clock – 8.00 a.m. She lay in bed, sulking, waiting for Elodea to ring back. "I expect she wants a lift somewhere," Priscilla said to herself. "It's my own fault. I should have told her that there definitely wasn't a bug on her car when I had the opportunity. Or pretended to remove it myself! Anything! I sometimes wonder if I have any brain at all these days! Being vulcanised before 9.00 a.m. is totally unacceptable! I must think of a reason why I can't go to Little Wychwell before she rings back. If it was term this would be simple. As it is… Maybe I could tell her I have a *funeral* to attend? Or a *wedding*? Or a meeting? But then she will ask me what meeting – bound to – which means I have to plan what sort of meeting before I say meeting. Whatever it is, I'm not getting up till she explains why she needs me!"

Priscilla snuggled down and was having a comfortable doze when her phone beeped again. She picked it up and stared blearily at the screen. It was a text from Elodea. Priscilla squinted at the little screen to try to make the words out.

"Don't bother. All OK," it said.

Good, thought Priscilla, settling back down into bed. She's found some other idiot to give her a lift. Probably having a lift in the post van!

It crossed her mind that the message from Elodea was strangely short. Usually Elodea's messages were more long, rambling and explanatory and took at least three txts to say anything at all. "She has finally learnt the art of brevity," she said to herself. She shut her eyes and composed herself for another nap when the phone beeped again. She kept her eyes firmly shut. But she couldn't settle. It was no good. She had to look.

"Smiths!" she said. "Vulcanisation! They should all be banned!"

"The person at the door was bringing Pippy back. She isn't lost! LoL O O O," said the next text.

"Ah!" said Priscilla, thinking that that explained why Elodea had seemed hysteric the first time. Elodea was *so silly* about that dog! 'LoL' must be a mistyped version of Elodea. Elodea never looked properly at the screen when she was typing, so she had somehow not hit the E hard enough and then pressed jkl instead of d, e and not hit that hard enough either. But why, wondered the non-txt proficient Priscilla, had Elodea put 'Oh, Oh, Oh!' at the end? Presumably O was short for Oh, like 'u' for 'you'? No, most likely Elodea had been absent-mindedly tapping on the 'O' button instead of pressing 'Send'. Priscilla was pleased with her own logic and finally concluded that, provided she herself was excused from rushing out to God-forsaken little villages to be vulcanised some more, she really didn't care how odd the message was.. Priscilla went straight back to sleep till her usual hour of rising, which was 10.00 a.m., and by that time she was not sure if the entire sequence of events had been a dream or real and cared less. Priscilla felt that her academic career filled her whole life quite sufficiently and, while she had been glad to see Barnabus and Elodea, she had now remembered the full inconvenient disadvantages of over close contact with Smiths, and decided to try and evade any attempted contact by the entire family for at least the next fortnight.

Chapter 8

Elodea had opened the door expecting to see the familiar face of Wayne, the postman. He would be ringing because he needed a signature on a parcel.

But it wasn't. It was a tall man who, at first, appeared to be a complete stranger.

"Detective Inspector Andrew Wright, Mrs Smith," he said.

Elodea hastily whisked him into the house and closed the door behind him.

"Flipper!" she cried, joyfully. "I *knew* you weren't dead! I just *knew* it!"

"Plan B," said a voice in Flipper's ear and added "*Women*!" followed by a gurgle of laughter, for the voice belonged to a woman.

"How did you know it was me?" asked Flipper's own voice. "I'm sure my *voice* was *perfect*! What a *waste* of plastic surgery!"

"You've had *plastic surgery*?" asked Elodea. "Was your nose the wrong size or something? I thought you looked fine before."

She stood back from him a little and considered his new appearance.

"Yes, yes, you do look a *bit* different," she said. "But I do hope you didn't *pay* them too much to do that surgery because you were *perfectly lovely* before; there was *absolutely no call for it*, no call for it *whatsoever*! I suppose these days you young men are as vain as young women. All this *equality*! And I see you've dyed your hair *blond*! I hope you don't mind me saying that it doesn't *suit* you, Flip, dear. You looked better dark-haired. God chooses our hair colour to go with our faces, I always think. Not *grey* though – no one is *meant* to have grey hair. *That is why hair dye exists*. And definitely no one should go white, *ever*!"

"Mrs Smith!" said Flipper, smiling at her quaint and earnest logic. "I don't think that I look anything like the way I used to!"

"Well, *no*, Dear. You are a lot *older* than you were when I last saw you. Men change so fast at your age. You go from young boys to adults and you never look the same again. I've noticed it with all my sons!" Elodea sighed. "They are all so grown-up now. You should see Barnabus! Or did you go to see him first? He will be so pleased!"

"Just for, er, just for the sake of it, tell me *how* you knew it was me?" said Flipper.

"Well, Flipper darling, you still have the same lovely *soul* and the same eyes that it shines out from, even if you are wearing coloured contact lenses. Those are so clever, don't you think? I suppose you wanted blue eyes to go with your blond hair! Again, though, I think you looked better with brown! But you see, plastic surgery and dye won't change your beautiful soul! And," she added, in case he was feeling upset because he had spent so much money and she wasn't impressed, "you are *very* good looking now, although you always were to *me* before," she cooed soothingly, for she did not want to disappoint him. Perhaps he had come to see her, thinking she would not recognise him, and was then going to say "Surprise, it's me: Flipper!" Men were such babies sometimes. She hoped he hadn't paid the surgeon too much though. To her way of thinking he was worse looking than he had been before, not better. Perhaps he didn't want to look like his parents. She seemed to recall something about them not getting on or some such story. No, she corrected herself, it wasn't that they didn't get on but that his parents were both dead – that was it! She felt guilty about having nearly forgotten that fact. Poor Flipper! Perhaps it had just been that he had gone a little wild after they both died. No, it couldn't be that either because they had died quite a few years ago.

Flipper gave up his attempts to find out the flaw in his new appearance. The laughter in his ear was getting too much.

"Anyway," Elodea continued, "I'm so glad you have turned up because I have a little problem, and if you are in the undercover police force these days – and I am making a big assumption that you are because that must be why you pretended to be dead – I think you might know how to fix it."

"What?" said Flipper.

"Although I have to say that even if it *is* because of your job, it was perfectly horrid of you to let Barnabus think you were dead, and Walls, and Finn. They were all very cut up about it. Barnabus was up at the cemetery visiting your grave only a day or two ago. I went to see it with him. It's a lovely grave but I suppose you find talking about it a bit macabre even if you aren't dead. I suppose they buried a coffin full of stones or something. So clever, all you undercover people! Am I allowed to tell Barnabus you are alive? Is that why you are here? You came to tell me to tell him you are alive so he can stop being sad?"

Flipper was beginning to feel that the whole conversation was now so far out of control that it might be impossible to ever get back to his intended purpose for the visit. He decided to ask about Elodea's "little problem" first. It could be something he needed to know about.

"So what is this little problem you have, Mrs Smith?" he asked.

"Do call me Elodea, now you are a grown-up adult. Everyone else does!" said Elodea.

"OK, OK, but what is the problem, Mrs, er, *Elodea*?" asked Flipper.

"Well, I don't suppose you know who she is but I know someone called Fran and she claimed that she had somehow put a tracking device on my car, and I want to know how to find it and get it off," said Elodea. At this point she remembered that Flipper was in the police and that she might get Fran into trouble, so she added, "She's a *friend* of mine. She put it on there for a *joke*. She bet me that I couldn't find it!"

"Mrs Smith," said Flipper, smiling down at her, "you are a shockingly untruthful woman! And also a very, very poor liar."

Elodea sighed. "I don't see how you can tell that!" she said – an echo of his earlier statements to her. "Anyway, for *whatever* reason she put it there, can you find it and take it off?"

"I will," said Flipper, "get our car decontamination squad out right away. They will check the whole car out. They will appear to be a windscreen replacement service, and, indeed they will also replace your windscreen. Just to make sure. I expect you have several chips given that you drive round on these roads, do you not?"

"Flipper, dear, you have no idea how *grateful* I am! The fact my car might be bugged has been troubling me just a *little*. Not that it was a *big* problem, nothing to complain about, but just a bit of a bother! And you are quite right: I have little blips all over the windscreen. Getting quite a hazard in the dark," said Elodea, and she then breathed in rapidly and continued, without stopping for more oxygen. "Now, did you come here looking for Barnabus? Because if so, he is at work, and, of course, he lives with Angel and the children now anyhow. But there is no one in their house right now either so there is no point in sending you round there to leave a message because Angel has taken the children up to visit her parents, and John is at work in Oxford as well, so there is only me here too." She paused again to take a quick gasp of air.

Flipper, recognising a chance, opened his mouth but before he could speak Elodea had plunged on again. "Barnabus – not that you call him that – *Buffy*, will be so happy to see you again! But you might do better to call round to *his* house on a *Saturday*, perhaps? You see, with him being at work all week and the two children – you do know about the children, don't you? – and Angel working such funny hours, it's difficult for him to do social things in the week at all now, poor boy!"

She stopped. Flipper, feeling quite breathless himself, but poised on the starting blocks this time, dashed in before she could resume yet again.

"I've not come to see Buffy, Mrs Smith, *Elodea*," he said, "and you *mustn't* tell Buffy that I've been here! The fact I am alive is a big secret, you understand. *You mustn't tell anyone*!"

"Oh!" said Elodea, sounding enormously disappointed. "I wish I could have told Barnabus. He is so sad about it, you know!"

"Well," said Flipper, "you can't. I'm so sorry but that is how it is. You mustn't tell anyone. Promise?"

"Promise!" said Elodea, dolefully. She sagged visibly and stopped talking and stood there, silent and sad, at the thought that she could not ease Barnabus' grief by explaining that the person he was mourning was still alive. How stupid!

"How fortunate it is that Barnabus *already knows*," said the voice in Flipper's ear. "She is bound to tell him. I knew we should have sent someone else round! I don't know why you insisted on doing this job."

I don't either really, thought Flipper to himself. I just suddenly missed the old times. I wanted my old life back, just for a few minutes, even if I had to pretend to be someone else. I wanted to feel younger and safer, just for a short time. I wanted to be a little boy at university again. I'm just stupid, he concluded. Stupid and sentimental.

"I've come to see *you*, you see!" said Flipper. "And I'm afraid I have some sad news to deliver."

"*John*!" screamed Elodea, changing from social to hysterical in one sudden flash. "Is he dead? Is he *dead*?"

"No, no, John is fine, to the best of my knowledge."

"*Paris*!" shrieked Elodea, louder and higher. "Obviously, it's Paris! *Paris*! *What happened*? *What happened*?"

"Paris is perfectly OK as well, as far as I know!" said Flipper.

He could see the start of the word "Elizabeth", her eldest child, forming on her lips and forestalled her before he suffered permanent ear damage as she worked through the entire family. He put one hand gently and kindly over her mouth.

"Nothing is wrong with any of your relatives, immediate or distant. They are all well. It's a friend of yours," said Flipper. He took his hand away.

"*Walls*!" was the prompt response, delivered at jet engine frequency.

"No, no, no!" said Flipper, reeling slightly at the volume and decibel level Elodea had now achieved, and then putting his hand very, very gently back over her mouth to prevent her reciting a list of friend's names. "No, not Walls! No, no, not a close friend even. But I think you might be sad. It's someone you just mentioned. I'm afraid I have some very bad news about Fran."

He took his hand away again. Was it safe now?

"*Fran*! *No*! *What's happened to her*? The poor thing! Not quite right in the head, you know, but she means well, I'm sure she does! Has she been *arrested*? She hasn't *killed* someone, has she?" yelled Elodea, but at a *slightly* lower and calmer level.

Flipper winced at the blast of noise.

"I'm glad you believe she always meant well – it shows a wonderful facet of your own character – but I am afraid that I may have to disillusion you about that. However, yes, there is very bad news. She was found floating in the Cherwell this morning, quite beyond resuscitation. I'm afraid she is definitely and unquestionably dead."

"*Dead*!" shrieked Elodea. "Her poor parents! Should I go round and see them? Do they need support, do you think? Can you imagine how they must feel? I'm sure she was a burden to them at times but for her to die, that is truly terrible! How dreadful! How very dreadful!"

A large tear rolled down her nose.

"And I had those photos of her and I didn't report it. I *killed* her, Flipper! I *killed* her! I should have reported those odd photos from yesterday. I could have saved her! I was *just about* to report the one from *last* night but it's all too *late*!" Elodea wailed. She sat down on one of the hall chairs, buried her face in her hands and burst into very loud sobs.

"No, no, Mrs Smith, *no one* could have saved her! *No one*!" said Flipper, patting her back gently in an awkward sort of way. "She had delivered herself into an unsolvable tangle and she knew perfectly well what she was doing and what the dangers were. You mustn't be so hard on yourself. She was trying to *kill* you, you know!"

"I know she tried to kill me once," said Elodea, rendered almost incoherent by her tears, so that Flipper had to bend towards her to catch what she was saying. "But that was a long time ago, and she didn't mean it, she didn't mean it – the alcohol, the drugs, her awful lifestyle. It wasn't her fault she was *not right*, you know!"

"Mrs Smith, *Elodea*, listen to me! I'm not talking about the first time she tried to kill you! Fran tried to have you assassinated *two days ago*! You remember the trip to the *cemetery*? She had hired a contract killer, and she took you to the cemetery herself to make sure he got the right target. You are very lucky to be alive! Have you got some tissues or anything around? Let's sort you out a little and then I can explain."

Flipper took an exploratory turn round the hall, considering different doors, and arrived in a room that had once been the kitchen but was now almost unidentifiable in its purpose due to a tidal wave of items that had been washed in from the rest of the house and never managed to flow back. Flipper found the table underneath a heaving and unstable pile of books, tins, magazines, unopened letters, bottles, jars and newspapers. He fished rather nervously among the piles and uncovered a roll of kitchen towel. He took it back and handed it to Elodea, who had now had time to digest his last speech. Elodea unwound a large chunk of kitchen towel, blew her nose loudly, dabbed at her eyes, coughed and then spoke again.

"Oh dear! That was very *naughty* of her! I suppose she was having *delusions* again? You see, she's bipolar or schizophrenic or psychopathic or something like that. She really can't *help* it!"

"I would offer to make you some tea but I don't think I'll be able to find my way round your kitchen. Perhaps," said Flipper, desperately, thinking the familiar action of making tea might calm her, "perhaps *you* could make us some tea and then we can sit in the lounge and have a little chat?"

"Oh, Flipper!" hiccupped Elodea, recovering almost instantly, springing off the chair and starting towards the kitchen, then turning back to speak to him. "I do apologise for being so remiss! I haven't offered you a drink since you arrived! How very rude of me! I'll get some tea and cake straight away and then we can sit in the lounge and talk about old times! It's not your fault you had to bring such bad news about Fran being dead! I'm so sorry. I suppose you get used to having to tell people that other people are dead in your job, but it must be very difficult for you! Have you got time for a chat? I'm not stopping you getting on with your work? Are you in a terrible hurry? I tend to forget how busy people are because of not having a paid job myself!"

Flipper sat down, rather heavily, on the chair that Elodea had vacated. "Yes, super, Mrs Smith, er, Elodea, no, it's fine, I've got plenty of time for a chat. It's my coffee break time right now!" he lied, rather desperately. "You go and get some tea and cakes, or coffee and cakes given the time, and then, yes, we can have a lovely little talk."

Perhaps if she has a mouth full of cake I might have more of a chance of talking, he said to himself.

"Coffee! Yes, yes! I'll have coffee too. It is elevenses time, after all," she said as she vanished into the kitchen. "So sorry; I should have offered you coffee, not tea, at this time of day! How silly of me! I'll go and get it all! Go and sit in the lounge instead. The door just behind you, Flipper, dear! I'm so sorry to cry. Don't think that I am not delighted to see you! I am! I'll be back in a jiffy! Oh, I must just send Priscilla a message. No point in her coming round now. All too late to do anything about Fran."

"Give me your phone!" said Flipper. "*I'll* send her the message, to save you the bother!"

"Yes, yes! I'm still a bit sniffy. I might not be able to see the screen properly. Getting older. Eyesight starts going, you know. Need to hold the phone miles away to see it at all. Tell her," said Elodea, "tell her that it's OK; she doesn't need to come round." She then added, with a piece of inspiration, "She didn't know why I wanted her to come round in the first place so tell her the caller at the door had brought Pippy back, so she isn't lost and I don't need any help!"

The end of the speech was muffled by distance. Flipper wandered into the lounge, looked very dubiously at the choice of sofas and chairs, all of which seemed to be exuding horsehair and kapok and even, in places, springs and spars of wood. He growled back at Pippy, who was growling at him in case he sat down on her by mistake, and lowered himself cautiously down into a faded blue disaster that the Smiths still called an armchair.

Elodea was a little calmer and her brain was running in a more orderly fashion by the time she reappeared.

"I did wonder," she said, humbly, "if Fran was up to anything the other day. But, you see, she told me that Barnabus was in danger, so, naturally, I never hesitated to go with her, even though I know she isn't trustworthy and I have been told by John and Barnabus to keep away from her. So don't tell either of them. Not that you will because they don't know you're alive so you can't. But Priscilla thought that what Fran said was true as well. She would be the first person to tell me not to do things like that but she did it herself. I suppose Fran is a psychopath so you can't really blame her for being born like that but you see that's the problem with psychopaths: they can persuade others so well because they believe what they are saying themselves! The whole thing was really very clever of her, you know. She even borrowed my phone so, I presume, she could tell the assassin we were going to the cemetery as well as her telling Barnabus, which was why she said she had borrowed it. I hope that isn't why you just borrowed my phone, Flipper darling. You aren't a psychopath as well, are you? I should have thought of that. Oh dear! I never learn. You aren't, are you? I suppose it might be quite useful in your profession. But maybe that isn't your profession. Now I'm scaring myself."

She smiled reassuringly at him so that he would know she was joking.

Flipper decided it was definitely unnecessary to even begin to explain that he himself and 'the doctor' had already been tracking Fran, Elodea and the hitman. Elodea was quite right, however: Fran had used Elodea's phone to tell the assassin they were on their way. Due to his own brilliance, he congratulated himself, Elodea's phone was also being tracked because she was a Facebook friend of Fran's. Otherwise they might not have got there in time.

"Yes, I'm afraid she was *up to something*, as you say," Flipper answered. "You see, she never, ever forgave you for the fact she thought Ustin was in love with you, and she continued to believe that that was why he had not remained faithful to her, not that he was ever in love with her. That was all her own delusion. As you said, her head was not at all right. She was, indeed, stalking you again."

"Well, I hope she finds peace now she is dead," said Elodea, wondering if it was at all Christian to have a little glad feeling inside that someone who has been trying to kill you is dead themselves, and then deciding it wasn't. "Maybe she is with Ustin again in heaven, and he can put her straight about not being in love with me, and they can be happy together there because people in heaven do not marry and are not given in marriage, just like angels, you know!"

Flipper spluttered into his cup and coughed.

"Coffee down the wrong way!" he gasped, weakly.

"I hope you don't mind me asking," continued Elodea, "but, but, *was* it Ustin that Walls and Barnabus found drowned in the river? And if it was, could I possibly, possibly tell Barnabus that he was right so he doesn't think he is going mad any more?"

"No, it wasn't Ustin," said Flipper, without turning a hair at this lie, "but it was *Ustin's identical twin brother*. He took over Ustin's gang activities, after Ustin, er, passed on."

"Ustin did drown then, all those years ago?" asked Elodea.

"*Presumably*," said Flipper, rather flippantly, "unless he is *very* good at swimming or unless someone else picked him up when he fell off the boat, which would be beyond unlikely since he fell off it in the middle of the Atlantic, or wherever the boat was. I can't remember where it was myself."

Flipper added, but only to himself, "But although this scenario *is* so *very* unlikely he *was* picked up, in fact he was picked up *from* the boat and persuaded to work for the other side, for the good guys, till he decided he loved money more than safety, and went back to playing his criminal games again."

"But," Flipper said out loud, "you *can't tell Barnabus, no*! And you can't tell him that I am still alive either, *remember*? In fact you can't tell him anything about me visiting or anything that I tell you."

"Oh!" said Elodea. "But Barnabus will be *so* unhappy if he never knows."

Flipper folded his lips sternly and did not reply.

"At least she'll tell Barnabus not to tell anyone else anything that she tells him now, and Barnabus will stop poking round investigating anything else himself. And if he tells Walls, it won't matter by this point in the investigation. They won't tell Angel or Yvette," said the voice in Flipper's ear.

"And," said Elodea, "the *hitman*? You did arrest him to make sure he doesn't shoot anyone else? Didn't you? And now he is in custody someone can explain to him why it's wrong to shoot people for money, and he can do something else, something honest, when he gets out."

Elodea did not even believe her last hopeful statement herself. She said a quick prayer that, whether she believed it or not, it might be true. What a dreadful life it must be: killing people just to get money. And she supposed once you started you couldn't really get out of it. She had seen a film a bit like that with George Clooney. It had been very sad and she had cried over it. John had told her she was an idiot. Elodea was not really listening to Flipper's reply or she might have thought a bit harder about the scene in the cemetery and realised what had actually happened.

"He got *picked up by some of our men*," said Flipper, with perfect truth.

"I know I shouldn't be grateful for the incarceration of another person and that the poor man must have had a lot of trauma in early life and it is so sad to be born as a psychopath, and you can hardly blame psychopaths for being born like they are, but I have to say that I *am* relieved to hear that!" said Elodea. "Because it must have made the world safer for *everyone else*, not just me. And he can get some proper psychiatric treatment while he is inside and then be released only when it's safe to do so!"

She smiled at her own lovely conclusion to the story.

Flipper managed to prevent a cynical expression appearing on his face at the thought of effective psychiatric treatment for prisoners or the possibility of psychopaths being 'cured'.

"Super! Yes!" he said.

"Oh!" said Elodea, who had returned to thinking about the cemetery. "The *old man*!"

"The *old* man?" asked Flipper, playing for time.

"I had *entirely* forgotten. There was an old man in the cemetery who had had a heart attack but there was a *lovely* doctor there looking after him. Barnabus saw him have the heart attack but we only arrived afterwards, and they took him off to hospital in an ambulance but I had meant to ring the John Radcliffe and see if he was there and if he was all right! I entirely forgot to do it! I must ring this afternoon and ask, as I expect he is still on one of the wards," said Elodea. "If it was a heart attack, that is. It could just have been indigestion, you know. That gets mistaken for a heart attack sometimes. Perhaps it was a stroke but if so he must have got to hospital well inside the four hours, so he should be OK."

"I don't think," said Flipper, quickly, "that hospitals will tell you *anything* down the *phone* these days, unless they are quite sure you are a *close relative*."

"So there's no point in ringing," said Elodea, disappointed. "Well, I shall just have to carry on keeping him in my prayers for a while."

"*Indeed*!" said Flipper, sounding *entirely* sincere. "But," he added, changing his voice to the solemn and slow tones which he thought appropriate for a bona fide detective inspector, "to return to the main reason for my visit – *Fran*. You said you had *some kind* of *photos* of *Fran*?"

"Oh, yes! Please tell me that you don't think it would have made any difference if I had told anyone about them yesterday. I do hope it wouldn't. I feel so *very, very guilty*!" Elodea replied, unrolling another wodge of kitchen towel and blowing her nose again.

"I *doubt* it, but maybe you could show them to me first and then I'll see what I think?" said Flipper. "When and how did you take these photos?"

Elodea explained to him, in a long muddled ramble, about the wildlife camera and Priscilla and everything else. Flipper listened to the entire story with great patience and did not yawn, not even once.

"Let's go and look at these photos then!" said Flipper, as Elodea finally concluded her ramblings.

"Ah!" he said when he had seen the first night's photos accompanied by Elodea's commentary.

Then "*Ah ha*!" when he had seen the second night's photos accompanied by Elodea's commentary.

Then "*Ah*!" again when he had seen the third night's photos and the running commentary was complete.

"And you say you *showed* some of these to Priscilla?" he asked.

"Yes. I took the first set in and showed them to her on *her* computer and she looked at the second night's here, but I was just going to get her to come out and see the third night's when you turned up," Elodea replied.

"Pretty harmless!" he said.

"Good," said the voice in Flipper's ear.

 "What?" asked Elodea.

"I don't think there is anything of any importance here. It wouldn't have made any difference even if you had reported them," said Flipper, smoothly. "As you thought, her parents came and collected her on both nights, but they had to give her a shot of sedative on the second one and then they had to carry her to the car after that. She isn't really bundled up; it's just this camera – the picture is very blurred. They're old, her parents. She is quite a weight for them to lift. I don't know how they managed it at all!"

"Silly me!" said Elodea. "I should have *realised* it was her *parents* on both nights! I expect she left a note telling them she was coming here or something of the sort. I suppose if she is being difficult they *do* have to give her a sedative, and then she would be *very* heavy to carry! What a *burden* for them both! At least they can get some better sleep now. But they must be *devastated* by her death! Do you think she went out when she was still a bit sedated? That might have caused her to wander into the river by mistake. You know, awake but not knowing what she was doing? Oh dear, how *terrible* for her parents if so! They will be thinking that if *only* they had sat beside her bed and watched over her till it had worn off —"

"Yes, I expect the sedative *may* have affected her judgment," interrupted Flipper.

"A fertile imagination is always a useful tool in this job," said the voice in his ear, "especially when the person you are talking to has one of her own and thus will not see the problem with such a ridiculous story!"

Flipper made a noise that was a sort of choking cough.

"Oh, how very unfortunate," said Elodea, leaping up and rushing round to pat him on the back. "I do hope it wasn't a cake crumb. Was your piece of cake a bit dry?

Mine was beautifully moist! Perhaps you had the one from the end? The edge could have been a bit…"

"I'm fine now! My cake was absolutely delicious!" Flipper assured her, before she embarked on the Heimlich manoeuvre. "Nothing wrong with the cake. Just bolting my food as usual! Greedy me!"

"But poor, poor Fran!" said Elodea. "She must have seen Ustin's brother on the towpath and thought it was Ustin. That explains that poem on Facebook: the one about the Lady of Shallot! Poor lovelorn Fran, so *alone*! If I'd only realised, I could have gone outside and spoken to her, when I saw her outside, you know!"

"It's as well you didn't," said Flipper. "Given her jealousy of you it wouldn't have helped, and she might have taken the opportunity to kill you on the spot, you know!"

"Oh, but she wouldn't have *meant* any harm, even if she had," cried Elodea. "She couldn't *help* not being quite right in the head! And perhaps I could have saved *her*…"

"Nobody could have saved her!" said Flipper quite sharply. Elodea was really taking Christianity too far, even if she didn't entirely mean what she actually said.

He stared at the computer screen silently for a few moments and then pressed some buttons on the keyboard.

"*My oh my*!" he said. "Did you know you've got a *nasty virus* on this machine?"

"I have? How did I get it? John will be *furious* with me! He's always telling me to be careful what I download or open. The virus checker hasn't said anything! Stupid thing! Oh dear! Oh dear! *What am I to do*? Is it *wiping all the data*?" gabbled Elodea, instantly completely distracted from her thoughts of Fran.

"Well, *you* know, hard to avoid them *all* the time. The *Internet*!" said Flipper, vaguely, but sympathetically. "*Packed* with the things! You can get them from *anywhere*. Just happens. Happens to everyone! Some of these viruses are so clever they evade the checks! Evil minds that design them, but also undeniably brilliant. Geniuses in their own field."

"Oh dear! John will be *so upset*!" said Elodea. "I expect I'll have to buy another computer to get rid of it, and that will be an *expense* and he will be very annoyed because this one is quite new really! And he might make me *throw away all my files*! I'll lose everything I have on this computer! It hasn't destroyed my photographs or anything yet, has it? Oh, how could I have been so *stupid*? I did open a spam email the other day by mistake. I expect it was that!"

"It's not *your fault*. Like I said, they just *get in*. Damn clever. But, don't worry; I can fix the problem!" said Flipper. "Or rather *I have a friend who can*; he's a computer whiz! I'll send him round this afternoon to fix it. Or heal it, or whatever they say! Called Rodney. Are you in *at around 2.00 p.m.?*"

"Yes, yes! You are sure he can fix it? I suppose he's one of your colleagues. I suppose you need to know all about this stuff in your job. That would be so very kind of you if he could *possibly* spare the time. I don't want to be an imposition on his time. If I'm not in just tell him he can let himself in through the back door. I always leave it unlocked. There's never any need to lock doors in Little Wychwell. We all let ourselves in and out of each other's houses all the time!" Elodea said, now happy and confident again.

"Yes, no, he's just a *friend* of mine, but he's a computer genius. He'll soon fix that problem. But you really should lock your back door for security reasons," said Flipper, resuming his detective inspector persona.

"Oh but then I would keep locking *myself* out! And Barnabus always forgets his keys as well! Apart from which there is no one at all likely to try coming in except my friends and family," said Elodea. "I do lock it *sometimes* if we go away or anything. I'll make quite sure I leave it open this afternoon!"

"Is this the wildlife camera you use?" asked Flipper, picking it up from the desk. "The one that isn't catching the animals at their games?"

"Yes, that's it! I always keep it by the computer when it's not in the garden, so as not to lose it!" said Elodea.

"If you are using *this* one then no wonder you aren't getting decent pictures," said Flipper. "This type is much too easy for the animals to detect. I'll get Rodney to bring you an old one of his own along – one that works much better. He was trying to give it to me the other day. Not my sort of thing at all though. He does a lot of wildlife observation himself," said Flipper, thinking that 'wildlife' was a quite good description for the sort of people that he and his friends usually set surveillance cameras to observe.

"A camera that works better? That would be *super*! But I must *pay* for it," said Elodea. "Rodney might not want to give it to me even if he was prepared to give it to you!"

"No, it's OK," said Flipper. "If you could just let Rodney have the other one as a swap? He likes to use them for spare parts to build his own photography equipment for doing, er, wildlife watching!"

"Inventive powers drying up?" asked the voice in his ear, sarcastically.

"Are you *sure*? I don't want you to be actually paying for it yourself. I have enough money to pay for it myself! And of course your friend can have the other one if he wants it. If he is being kind enough to heal that virus and give me his old camera then that is the least I can do," said Elodea.

"Was that the *only* way you could think of getting hold of that camera card and erasing the photos and evidence from her computer?" asked the voice in his ear. "Very well, I'll sort an old surveillance camera out for her! But no more unauthorised gifts, young man!"

"Now just *don't use the computer at all until Rodney's been*! I can't answer for what might happen to your files if you do!" said Flipper.

"I must remember to tell him his latest name," said the voice in his ear. "He's going to just *love* being *Rodney*!"

"That is so very, very, kind!" said Elodea, bestowing upon him one of her delicious smiles. He had forgotten how lovely Buffy's mother was. She didn't look old enough to be *anyone's* mother when she smiled. He smiled back at her and she, suddenly seeing him as a vulnerable and lost little boy, gave him a big hug and kissed him on the cheek.

"I must cut now!" he said to her, confused for a moment and forgetting his solemn detective demeanour entirely. "Lots to do!"

"Such a shame you can't stay longer," said Elodea. "You must come again!"
She remembered that his own mother and father were dead and felt sad for him. He must get lonely with no

family. "Any time you like! I always have some cake in the tin!"

Elodea went to the door with Flipper, but then told him to wait while she ran back to the kitchen to cut a very large wedge of cake. She wrapped it up in a piece of foil and tucked it into his pocket "for later". She stood on tiptoe and gave another him a big motherly kiss and a hug. *Poor* Flipper: even more alone than Fran! Not just his parents being dead either. She had remembered that he was himself 'dead' too. Poor boy! What an awful life!

"Yes, I'll pop back some time!" he said to her, sounding confident while actually thinking that this event was *most* unlikely.

"Yes, yes, do!!" she said.

She gave him another big motherly hug and he turned and left.

Thank goodness, he said to himself, as he slipped away down the lane, that the world was *not* run by people like Elodea. For if it was it would be a terrible and anarchic place in which bad people were excused any criminal actions, including murders or torture or even massacres of the innocent, on the grounds that they had had a difficult childhood, or were a bit upset at breakfast time.

What a fortunate thing for Elodea and her ilk that people like him were around. Otherwise they would all be most certainly be dead themselves. Elodea most definitely would not have survived this incident. He reflected back on the tangled case that she had managed to stumble into. Firstly Ustin, who *was*, of course, the man in the river. 'Our side' had collected him from Lady Wilmington's yacht and recruited him, on pains of being killed otherwise, and he had done some sterling work clearing up drug traffickers for a while. But the lure of the big money earned from drug trafficking had been too much for him and he had given his minder the slip and returned to the underworld. Then he had resurfaced in Oxford. When Flipper had cornered him near the Cherwell things had got so much more complicated. Although, thought Flipper, better that *he* got shot than that *I* did! The scene replayed in his mind. Ustin had been 'difficult'. Flipper managed to get his own arms round Ustin so that Ustin's arms were pinned to his sides, but Ustin had managed to pull the pair of them backwards and into the Cherwell. Flipper had been forced to let go of Ustin's arms to avoid them both drowning. The danger of being shot by Ustin, who could now get at his gun, had been sufficient for Flipper to have fill in on his report the usual fiction about "the apprehended criminal having then shot himself in the head". After shooting Ustin in the head Flipper was then seriously off balance in the water himself and it was only with a struggle that he had regained the bank. Unfortunately they had been close to the junction with the Isis, and Ustin's body had floated straight out into it. Even worse, there were no nearby boats to purloin temporarily and Flipper had been forced to make a large detour to cross the Isis at Folly Bridge in order to run down the towpath and relocate the lost body. Given the weather and lack of people this should still have been OK. But that, as he said to himself, was where the whole affair had really been screwed up: stupid river not having an available rowing boat or a bridge nearer the junction; stupid friends turning up and heaving bodies out of rivers! Just when the wonderful wet weather should have meant there was no one around, Walls and Barnabus had to turn up! Not just turn up but actually fish the body out of the river before himself or his back-up could get there. Incredible!

However, it had been very lucky for Elodea that he and his colleagues had been monitoring Fran as soon as they knew Ustin was back in the area, because of her previous connections with him, not really thinking that any contact between the two was likely these days. She had seemed to be entirely reformed and being kept well under control by tranquilisers and her parents anyway. But the monitoring had turned out to be more exciting than anyone expected as they had discovered that Fran *was* the 'Red King': a big international drug dealer from the Dark Web, who they had been hunting for many months. No one had imagined that Fran's fuddled brain was capable of using the Dark Web or of running such a massive and successful illegal business. Her apparently reformed and restricted life had fooled everyone. In any case, as one of Flipper's own colleagues had said, how were they meant to realise that someone calling themselves the Red *King* was a *woman*, eh, what?

Even more fortunately, they were monitoring Elodea because, following their suspicion of who the Red King might be – unlikely as the identification still seemed – they were monitoring all Fran's Facebook friends.

"And people say monitoring people secretly is wrong," said Flipper to himself, with satisfaction at the falsity of this idea. "I bet Elodea thinks secret monitoring is wrong herself! Well, she'd be dead otherwise! I don't expect thanks though. I can be happy just by being right and doing a good job!"

He sighed aloud with pleasure at his own usefulness and brilliance.

Ustin had reappeared in the area because his own Dark Web drug dealing was being encroached upon by the Red King, and he had managed to track down the unknown's geographical location to Oxford. Fran had then spotted Ustin, quite by chance, on the   towpath. But even though Fran was running a whole illegal operation so successfully, she was still very mentally unstable. Seeing Ustin had firstly revived Fran's obsessional love for him, then reminded Fran of how much she hated Elodea, and finally convinced her that Elodea was going to try and 'steal' Ustin from her 'again'. Ustin had only the vaguest memories of Fran, who had seemed of little importance or consequence to him at the time, and, if he noticed her at all, did not even recognise her. For she was now clean, neat and expensively dressed and did not look at all like a down-and-out.

So Fran had started to stalk Elodea again, and planned her death. This time it was going to be a *certain* death, for Fran decided to use a hired assassin who would not botch things and who would not be traceable to herself. Fran did not want to risk prison again just when things were going so well. Her drug income made the expense no problem for her. Flipper's comrades had discovered through their ceaseless and meticulous monitoring that Fran had hired a hitman and also, only just in time, that Elodea was the target. "Bit of a close shave," Flipper said to himself.

Flipper had then been obliged to check with Barnabus that Elodea was, definitely, all above board herself. Not likely to be anything else but *you never knew*. If criminals all *looked* criminal, life would be so simple! Really big names in drug trafficking always hid in plain sight, usually further up in 'high society' than Elodea and Priscilla, but all the same, you *never knew*.

Ustin's gang, even without Ustin, were also homing in on Fran, for there are always people willing to sell information if the price is high enough.

Flipper and another operative had intercepted her in Little Wychwell and she had been offered a hefty bribe, immunity from arrest and a safe sanctuary from Ustin's gang in return for giving them the information they wanted. Once they had finished interrogating her they had installed her in a safe house en route to a new identity and a new life, having told her parents she had temporarily been admitted to inpatient mental health care and that no visits were advisory for the present. But Fran's fixation with Elodea was now so great that she had escaped from the safe house and returned to her nighttime vigil in Little Wychwell. This had been a major error of judgement, for some of Ustin's men had traced her there, drowned her and dumped her in the river.

What a good thing I haven't suffered any such irrational obsessive behaviour towards Audrey since she left me to marry that fat old senator, thought Flipper. But I don't give a *damn* about her! Better alone in this job. *Always better alone*. Love is just a distraction and a nuisance!

The voice in his ear broke into his thoughts. "Shame Elodea is almost bound to tell Barnabus that they were after her and not him, because then he can stop using all those lovely evasion tactics every time he takes a journey. He can even stop double-locking the front door." The voice laughed.

Flipper was in his car by now.

"It's been *so* funny. You should have seen him in Broad Street yesterday. A car backfired and I've never seen anyone hit the deck so quickly. Faster than a speeding bullet, as the phrase goes! Let alone all the slipping into shop doorways and checking right and left before he continues, and crawling around under his car to check for bombs! I do hope she doesn't tell him for at least the next few days. It's such a shame to spoil the fun!" said Flipper.

The voice laughed again. "But you must be more careful, Flip," it said, severely. "You know that. We shouldn't have got into the whole Ustin mess in the first place!"

"But it led to us rescuing Elodea. An innocent saved. It wasn't *all* bad!" he protested.

"I'm not sure we can justify that kind of expense for the sake of one woman!" said the voice, using its officious official tone.

"Nonsense!" protested Flipper. "There was hardly any expense. As errors go it was quite cheap!"

"Cheap?" said the voice. "You have a funny idea of cheap! You know how tight the budgets are these days!" It then added silkily, "We don't want to have to reduce our operatives now, do we?"

"No, Ma'am!" said Flipper, humbly and formally.

"New instructions. Return to base to file your reports immediately," the voice continued, also adopting a formal tone. "You have now completed your required involvement in this case."

Writing reports, thought Flipper, pooh-ey! Fabrication was *so* exhausting.

"And then you have a change of climate to look forward to," said the voice.

"Somewhere hot?" said Flipper, hopefully.

"Not the *hottest* place in the world," said the voice. "The Arctic. You are beginning a lovely new job with an oil exploration company in two days' time."

"*Super*!" said Flipper. They couldn't be that cross with him then. A new case! He cast all thoughts of Little Wychwell, Fran, the Smiths, Walls, Oxford and Finn from his mind. He put his foot down on the accelerator and sped off towards London. Once the tedious bit of report writing was over there would be a new challenge, a new place, new people. That was what he loved about this job: never bored and always that extra spice of danger!

In the Old Vicarage Elodea was sitting on a hall chair and praying for "poor Flipper". She supposed he had chosen that strange career because of both his parents dying so young. That would have affected anyone badly. Elodea really feared that Flipper *wasn't quite right in the head*.

Then she remembered that Fran was *dead*. She knelt down on the hard hall carpet, to pray for her soul.

She was so absorbed that she did not hear the back door open. But a thundering of little feet pounding towards her and loud cries of "Where are you, Nonna?" alerted her to the fact her house had been invaded.

She did not have time to finish rising from her knees and was in a position of very unstable equilibrium when Elodeus and Jasmine crashed into her. The three of them keeled over with a crash, landing on the floor unhurt but in a rugby scrum of struggling hugs and kisses.

Elizabeth, Elodea's eldest child and the children's mother, progressed towards the unruly heap in a more stately fashion.

"I'll leave them here then and go straight to Oxford, Mama!" Elizabeth pronounced. But Elodea's ears were partly muffled by bits of Jasmine and Elodeus.

"What did you say, Darling? I couldn't quite catch it!" Elodea yelled, at a volume that rose above the children's triumphant cries of "We love you!"

"I said... Oh, for goodness sake, *all of you*! Get off the floor and stop being so silly!" said Elizabeth, exasperated.

Rebuked, the children and Elodea sorted themselves out and got up.

"I do apologise. I can't stop even for a minute. I must get on to the epidemiology conference, Mama!" Elizabeth said. "The traffic was terrible on the way down! I must go *immediately*!"

"Dear me!" said Elodea, anxiously. "I do hope you haven't missed any sessions already. You haven't missed giving a speech, have you?"

"No. It's not starting officially till tomorrow, but I must be there to *network* with other people this afternoon. I'll be back in three days to collect. I'll grab their bags from the car for you and be gone!" Elizabeth said, sounding efficient and important and sweeping back out of the house again.

She marched in again, dumped three large holdalls on the hall floor, checked her watch, blew kisses at all of them and left peremptorily. Elodea sometimes wished that Elizabeth did not make her feel quite so much like a bothersome patient who was extending the appointment beyond anything desirable, much as she loved her only daughter.

Elodeus reappeared from a quick exploration of the downstairs of the house.

"You haven't got us any drinks and biscuits ready!" he said, accusingly. "I just checked the table. Nor any lunch in the oven! Had you *forgotten* we were coming?" he asked, looking closely and suspiciously at his grandmother's face.

"No, Darling! Of *course* I hadn't! How could I forget?" Elodea lied.

He glared at her, with a penetrating and disillusioned stare.

"You shouldn't lie!" he said. "Daddy Granny says you'll go to *hell* if you lie!"

"*No*, Elodeus!" corrected his sister. "Daddy Granny didn't say that *Mummy Granny* would go to hell if *she* lied. Daddy Granny said that *you* would go to hell if *you* kept telling such shocking whoppers about having done your homework when you hadn't even started it!" She gave Elodea a big hug. "You would *never* go to hell, Mummy Granny! You are too good and too kind!"

"Thank you, Jasmine darling," said Elodea, "but you are horribly right, Elodeus. I, I *had* forgotten you were coming today! It's been a bit busy lately what with one thing and another."

"Quite a lot of anothers," she said to herself.

Elodea continued, "But I hadn't forgotten you were coming completely! I had put it on the calendar; I remember doing it! It is so lovely to have you here! We can have such fun!"

"Fun! I should *think so*!" said Jasmine. "You are taking us to the Cotswold Wildlife Park today!"

"I am?" said Elodea.

"Oh yes!" said Jasmine. "We have it all planned out! The whole timetable for our visit. And *we* are going to help you look after Amadeus and Theodora as well! We are *all* going to go out *every day*! We are going to visit *everywhere*, and they are going to come *too*!"

"*Everywhere*?" said Elodea, feeling suddenly weak, and also thankful that Amadeus and Theodora were not back till tomorrow.

"Yes. *Tomorrow* you are taking us to *Blenheim Palace*!" said Elodeus. "We have the complete itinerary for all three days, planned to the last minute!"

Elodeus produced a sheet of paper from his pocket and waved it at his grandmother.

"See," said Jasmine, "the three of us, *five* with Amadeus and Theodora, are going to have *a tremendous time*!"

"I'm sure we are!" said Elodea, smiling down at her.

And Flipper shot backwards into the 'dear but miscellaneous' drawer at the back of her memory as the 'dear and much loved close relatives' drawer was catapulted to its proper place at the front. Flipper had, however, been refiled and relabelled and was no longer in the 'dear but miscellaneous and also now dead' file.

Fran had been downgraded into the 'miscellaneous and I know I should think they are dear because of what the Good Lord says but sometimes I find it hard, however I try, and now dead' drawer. But for just a moment the drawer flung itself open again as Elodea thought that she must find out when Fran's funeral was to take place and that she must go to it even if Elodeus and Jasmine and Amadeus and Theodora *were* with her on that day. Then she realised there was a very simple solution to that problem. Priscilla did not like Fran enough to want *go* to the funeral so Elodea could leave all four children with Priscilla, and Priscilla could take them round the Ashmolean or whatever. Fortunately for the sake of their continued friendship, Elodea was so distracted by the antics of Jasmine and Elodeus that she did not stop to text this delightful plan to Priscilla, and in the end it was never necessary to put it into practice.

Then Fran's presence vanished entirely from Elodea's mind as Jasmine and Elodeus gambolled and frolicked through the day. Humans are much more like grazing ruminant herds than we would usually admit. Just as zebras and wildebeest soon return to quiet grazing once the lions have made their kill, so we must do the same.

Barnabus was not currently quietly grazing, or rather not currently working to achieve money to graze, even though he was in his office. He was sitting at his desk but doing nothing at all except stare with a huge beaming smile at his iPhone. He had just received a text message from Angel to say that they were expecting *another* baby. The test had confirmed their suspicions. Will it be a girl or a boy this time, I wonder? he thought to himself, and followed this with: Mama will be *so* pleased! She does *love* looking after the babies so much! What a treat for her!

Barnabus abandoned his desk, murmuring an inaudible excuse to his neighbour, which he hoped would be interpreted as his having to leave to attend an urgent and important meeting. Then he slipped outside into the street, found a quiet corner and rang his wife to tell her how very, very much he loved her and how ecstatically happy he was.

Appendix

Quotations and phrases used in Little Wychwell Mystery Novels 1-6 - with translations if not in English

The author does not guarantee that this list is comprehensive, it is entirely possible that some phrases may exist in the novels which are not included here. She also does not guarantee the accuracy of the quotations, or of their translations or attributions. Especially since spellcheckers sometimes gratuitously 'correct' Latin words into entirely the wrong English word and the author has been known not to notice this.

··

1) LATIN QUOTATIONS – LISTED ALPHABETICALLY

A bove majori discit arare minor.

From the older ox, the younger learns how to plough

Abundans cautela non nocet – an overdose of caution does no harm

Abyssus abyssum invocat

Hells calls hell (Psalm 41:8 from the Vulgate translation of the Bible)

Acta deos numquam mortalia fallunt (Ovid) – the actions of mortals never deceive the gods.

Ad astra per alia porci – to the stars on the wings of a pig - This is an extension of the phrase 'ad astra', to the stars. Attributed to John Steinbeck.

Ad perpetuam rei memoriam – for the perpetual remembrance of the thing

Aequam memento rebus in ardis servare mentem   Remember that when life's path is steep you must keep your mind even – i.e. keep calm in the face of overwhelming odds.

Amo ut invenio – I love as I find – used as Amat ut invenit - he loves as he finds, insincere love of the sort that Walls is constantly displaying.

Amantes sunt amentes Lovers are mad

Ante victoriam ne canas triumphum. Do not sing your triumph before the victory.

THE AENEID Book 1 verses 1-11

Arma virumque cano, Troiae qui primus ab oris
Italiam, fato profugus, Laviniaque venit
litora, multum ille et terris iactatus et alto
vi superum saevae memorem Iunonis ob iram;
multa quoque et bello passus, dum conderet urbem,
inferretque deos Latio, genus unde Latinum,
Albanique patres, atque altae moenia Romae.

Musa, mihi causas memora, quo numine laeso,
quidve dolens, regina deum tot volvere casus
insignem pietate virum, tot adire labores
impulerit. Tantaene animis caelestibus irae?

I sing of arms and the man, who, exiled by fate,

first came from the coast of Troy to Italy, and to

Lavinian shores – thrown about endlessly by land and sea,

by the will of the gods, by remorseless Juno's anger,

suffering long in war, until he founded a city

and brought his gods to Latium: from this the Latin people

came, the lords of Alba Longa, they who built the walls of noble Rome.

Muse, tell me the cause: how was [Juno] offended in her divinity, how was she so upset, the Queen of Heaven, to drive a man,

a man who was renowned for virtue, to endure such dangers, to face so many

trials? Can there be such anger in the minds of the gods?

Arrectis auribus (Virgil) with ears pricked up.

ars gratia artis – art for arts sake

Assiduus usus uni rei deditus et ingenium et artem saepe vincit. (Cicero)

Constant practice devoted to one subject often outdoes both intelligence and skill.

Aut viam inveciam aut faciam – I'll either find a way or make one

bonum vinum laetificat cor hominis
Good wine gladdens a person's heart

brevis spem nos vetat incohare longam (Horace), Life is so short that we cannot cling to far off hope

Caesar si viveret, ad remum dareris - If Caesar were alive, you'd be chained to an oar

Castigat ridendo mores, (Jean de Santeul) you can correct customs by ridiculing them

Cave ab homine unius libri - Beware of anyone who has only one book.

Cave quid dicis, quando, et cui -Beware of what you say, when and to whom

Cave tibi cane muto, aqua silente. - Beware of the silent dog and the still water.

Carpe diem, quam minimum credula postero (Horace)- Seize the day, trust as little as possible in tomorrow

Cineri gloria sera venit (Martial) Fame after death (literally 'Fame to ashes') comes too late

Cito maturum cito putridum, early ripe, early rotten - precocious children will be troublesome later

Cogito summere potum alterum – I think therefore I'll have another drink

Conscientia mille testes - conscience is worth a thousand witnesses

Corpora lente augescent cito extinguuntur (Tacitus)– bodies grow slowly but die fast

cuiusvis hominis est errare, nullius nisi insipientis in errore perseverare (Cicero) Anyone can err, but only the fool persists in his fault

Damna minus consulta movent (Juvenal) Losses to which we are accustomed affect us less deeply.

data venia - literally means 'with all due respect' but is used before disagreeing.

De mortuis nil nisi bonum (Horace) only speak good of the dead

Disiderantem quod satis est neque tumultuosum sollicitat mare, non verberatae grandine vineae fundusque mendax (Horace)

He who desires only what is enough, is not troubled when seas rage, or when hail smites his vineyard, or if his farm has an unproductive year

Eheu fugaces labuntur anni (Horace)- Alas, the fleeting years slip by.

The full quotation for this is ….

Eheu fugaces, Postume, Postume, labuntur anni, nec pietas moram, rugis et instanti senaectae, adferet indomitaeque morti (Horace)

Alas, Postumus, the fleeting years slip by, nor will piety give any stay to wrinkles and pressing old age and untameable death.

Equo ne credite, Teucri. quidquid id est, timeo Danaos et dona ferentes (Virgil)

Do not trust the horse, Trojans, Whatever it is, I fear the Grecians, even bearing gifts

Eram quod es, eris quod sum - I was what you are, you will be what I am. (inscription on a grave)

Est modus in rebus (Horace) there is a middle ground

Est quaedam flere voluptas (Ovid) - There is a certain pleasure in weeping.

Et supposition nil ponit in esse – saying [or suggesting] something doesn't make it true

Experientia docet (Tacitus) experience teaches, 'you learn from experience', Priscilla is applying this with rather double meaning

Fabas indulcet fames – Hunger sweetens the beans, i.e all food tastes good when hungry

Familia supra omnia – family over everything else

Felix qui potuit rerum cognoscere causas (Virgil) Happy is he who can discover the causes of things

Festina lente – hurry slowly, i.e. more haste less speed

Fructu non foliis arborem aestima. Judge a tree by its fruit, not by its leaves.

Hic locus est ubi mors gaudet succurrere vitae – This is the place where death delights in helping life (*more usually used on pathological laboratories and similar places – Flipper is referring to his own supposedly dead state)*

In alio pediculum, in te ricinum non vides (Petronius) You see a louse on someone else, but not even a tick on yourself

(Erasmus) - In the country of the blind the one eyed man is king

lupus in fabula (Terence) – literally translates as 'the wolf in the story' but is generally interpreted as "speak of the wolf, and he will come" Terence was a Roman playwright who used this phrase in his play Adelphoe

malis mala succedunt – troubles are followed by troubles

Manebo semper fidelis ad locum nativitatis, Fidus ero prae ceteris omnibus locum nativitatis, Promitto vobis - **The loyalty oath of the boggart dancers though not necessarily accurate Latin -** I will remain ever faithful to the place of birth
in preference to others, I will be loyal to that place of birth
I promise you

Mendacem memorem esse oportet - It is necessary for a liar to be a man of good memory

Mens sana in corpore sano (Juvenal) a healthy mind in a healthy body

But what Juvenal actually said was

> It is to be prayed that the mind is healthy in a healthy body.
>
> Ask a brave soul who lacks the fear of death,
>
> who places the length of life last among the blessings that nature gives,
>
> who is able to bear any kind of suffering,
>
> who does not know anger, lusts for nothing and believes
>
> that the suffering and hard labours of Hercules are better than
>
> the pleasures, feasts, and feather bed of an Eastern king.
>
> I will tell you the gift you are able to give to yourself;
>
> It is certain that the only path you can follow to a tranquil life
>
> lies through virtue.
>
> orandum est ut sit mens sana in corpore sano.
>
> fortem posce animum mortis terrore carentem,
>
> qui spatium uitae extremum inter munera ponat
>
> naturae, qui ferre queat quoscumque labores,
>
> nesciat irasci, cupiat nihil et potiores
>
> Herculis aerumnas credat saeuosque labores

et uenere et cenis et pluma Sardanapalli.

monstro quod ipse tibi possis dare; semita certe

tranquillae per uirtutem patet unica uitae.

Nemo liber est qui corpore servit (Seneca) No one is free who is a slave to his own physical desires, Seneca

Nemo repente fuit turpissimus (Juvenal) no one ever became thoroughly evil in one step

Nil ego contulerim iucundo sanus amico (Horace)- While I am sane I shall compare nothing to the joy of a friend.

Nomen est omen – a name holds portentous meaning

Non est ad astra mollis e terris via – (Seneca) – there is no easy way from the earth to the stars, Priscilla uses this because Ustin has 'died' at least twice

Non ignara mali miseris succurrere disco (Virgil) - Being no stranger to misfortune myself, I have learned to relieve the sufferings of others non mihi, non tibi, sed nobis -Not for you, not for me, but for us

nullum magnum ingenium sine mixture dementiae fuit – There has been no great wisdom without an element of madness

numquam minus solus quam cum solus - never less alone than when alone

paruola ne nigras horrescat Erotion umbras, oraque Tartarei prodigiosa canis. (Martial)

May little Erotion not fear the dark shades nor the vast mouths of the Tartarean dog

Part of Martial's epitaph to a slave girl, who died aged 5, which Barnabus adapts by putting Priscilla in instead of Erotion

Pelle sub agnina latitat mens lupine – beneath the lamb's skin lurks a wolf's mind

Pendant opera interrupta – (Virgil) – the work is in limbo due to being interrupted

per angusta ad augusta Through difficulties to honour

Per ardeus ad astra – through the thorns to the stars

Periculum in mora – danger in delay

Piscem nature docem – teach fish to swim – Erasmus believed this saying was originally Greek

Plenus annis abiit, plenus honoribus! – (Pliny) – he has gone from us, full of years, full of honours

Pons asinorum – bridge of asses – an obstacle that is hard to cross for stupid people

Pol! – by Pollux! (short interjection used by Priscilla on hearing of the marriage of Tony and Flic.

Possunt quia posse videntur – they can because they seem able to – positive thinking can get you anywhere (Elodea is annoying Priscilla on purpose)

Post hoc ergo propter hoc – after this, therefore because of this (a logical error due to a person assuming that the first thing causes the second)

Proprium humani ingenii est odisse quem laeseris - It is human nature to hate a person whom you have injured

Pueri, pueri, pueri puerilia tractant – children are children therefore children do childish things

Quem di diligunt, adolescens moritur (Plautus translated from Menander who wrote it in Greek). - Whom the gods love dies young

Qui bibit, dormit; qui dormit, non peccat; qui non peccat, sanctus est; ergo qui bibit sanctus est

Who drinks sleeps, who sleeps does not sin, who does not sin is blessed, therefore those who drink are blessed

Qui totum vult totum perdit! (attrib to Seneca) he who wants everything loses everything

Quidquid agas prudenter agas. Whatever you do, do with caution.

The full proverb is Quidquid agas prudenter agas et respice finem i.e. Whatever you do, do with caution, and look to the end.

Quidquid Latine dictum sit altum videtur – anything that is said in Latin sounds profound

Quieta non movere. Don't disturb things that are at peace; i.e- Let sleeping dogs lie or Don't mend things unless they are broken.

Quod erat demonstrandum – literally 'which had to be demonstrated' and put at the end of a mathematical proof, as QED, but more generally used as 'that proves it!'

Quod gratis asseritur, gratis negatur – what is asserted without reason may be denied without reason

Quod me nutrit me destruit (ascribed to Christopher Marlowe) What nourishes me also destroys me

Retine vim istam falsa enim dicam si coges – restrain your strength for if you compel me I will tell lies (an utterance by the Delphic Oracle, originally in Greek)

Rides si sapis – (Martial) – laugh if you are wise

Risum tenatis amici – Can you help laughing, my friends?

Scio me nihil scire (Socrates or possibly Plato) - I know that I know nothing. (one cannot know anything with absolute certainty)

Si bene commemini, causae sunt quinque bibendi; hospitis adventus, praesens sitis, atque future, aut vini bonitas, aut quaelibet altera causa : Père Sermond

If I remember correctly there are five excuses for drinking, the visit of a guest, thirst right now, thirst due in the future, the quality of the wine or any other reason you choose.

Si hoc legere scis nimium eruditionis habes - if you can read this, you're overeducated (Flipper's reply to Priscilla who had quoted Socrates - Scio me nihil scire)

Si vis pacem para bellum – if you want peace you must prepare for war

Sum ergo edo – I am therefore I eat

sumus semper in excretum sed alter variat. We are always in the muck, only the depth varies – although this Latin may be questionable

Spero nos familiares mansuros - I hope we'll still be friends

Studium immane loquendi   an insatiable desire for talking

Tanta stultitia mortalium est – Such is the foolishness of mortals

Tempus edax rerum – time consumes everything, essentially means the same as tempus fugit. (Which is why Priscilla rephrases it to this when tempus fugit, time flies, makes Elodea giggle and launch into "fruit flies like a banana")

Tempus fugit – time flies

Timidi mater non flet - a coward's mother does not weep

Tu ne cede malis sed contra audentior ito – do not surrender to misfortunes but advance boldly against them

Ut biberet quoniam esse nollet – (*Publius Claudius Pulcher before the battle of Drepana as he threw the sacred chickens which had refused to eat grain, a sign of bad luck, overboard, recorded by Cicero and Suetonius*) so that they might drink since they refuse to eat

Ut Roma cadit sic omnis terra – as Rome falls so falls the whole world

Viva enim mortuorum in memoria vivorum est posita (Cicero)– The dead are kept alive in the memory of the living.

2) <u>SOME OF THE ENGLISH QUOTATIONS WHICH ARE REFERRED TO IN ALL THAT GLISTERS IS NOT SILVER</u>

O hell! what have we here?
A carrion Death, within whose empty eye
There is a written scroll! I'll read the writing.
All that glisters is not gold;
Often have you heard that told:

Many a man his life hath sold
But my outside to behold:
Gilded tombs do worms enfold.
Had you been as wise as bold,
Young in limbs, in judgment old,
Your answer had not been inscroll'd:
Fare you well; your suit is cold.

(Shakespeare, the Merchant of Venice)

I consider as lovers of books not those who keep their books hidden in their store-chests and never handle them, but those who, by nightly as well as daily use thumb them, batter them, wear them out, who fill out all the margins with annotations of many kinds, and who prefer the marks of a fault they have erased to a neat copy full of faults. (Erasmus on books)

 For all sad words of tongue and pen, The saddest are these, It might have been (John Greenleaf Whittier)

Modern man likes to pretend that his thinking is wide-awake. But this wide-awake thinking has led us into the mazes of a nightmare in which the torture chambers are endlessly repeated in the mirrors of reason (Octavio Paz).

Outside of a dog, a book is man's best friend. Inside of a dog it's too dark to read. (Groucho Marx)

Wanted: a dog that neither barks nor bites, eats broken glass and shits diamonds (ascribed to Goethe)

I have shown you the methods that lead to liberation but you should know that liberation depends upon yourself. (Buddha)

'Remember that not getting what you want is sometimes a wonderful stroke of luck!" Dalai Lama

I believe that the very purpose of our life is to seek happiness. That is clear. Whether one believes in religion or not, whether one believes in this religion or that religion, we are all seeking something in life. So, I think, the very motion of our lives is towards happiness. Dalai Lama

3) **QUOTATIONS IN SPANISH**

A quien madruga, Dios le ayuda. God helps those who get up early.

Por mucho madrugar, no amanece mas temprano. Day dawns none the sooner because we rise early.

4) **QUOTATIONS IN ANGLO SAXON**

verses 92-102 from chapter 2 of the Anglo Saxon version of Genesis A.

> þa þeahtode þeoden ure
> modgeþonce, hu he þa mæran gesceaft,
> eðelstaðolas eft gesette,
>
> swegltorhtan seld, selran werode,
> þa hie gielpsceaþan ofgifen hæfdon,
> heah on heofenum. Forþam halig god
> under roderas feng, ricum mihtum,
> wolde þæt him eorðe and uproder
>
> and sid wæter geseted wurde
> woruldgesceafte on wraðra gield,
> þara þe forhealdene of hleo sende.

Which translates roughly as

Then our Lord took counsel in his innermost heart as to how He might fill, with a better set of candidates, the great creation, the native seats and gleaming mansions, high in heaven, from which these boasting foes had come forth. Therefore with his mighty power Holy God ordained, that in the earth and the sky and the huge sea, that lay below these wide stretching heavens, earth-creatures should appear, as a replacement for those rebels whom He had cast out of heaven.

Made in the USA
Charleston, SC
25 March 2014